WANDERING HOME

Susan Lamanna Verzulli

Purple Owl Publishing
7 Kingman Rd
Newton, MA 02461

To my family

PART I
GUILLAUME

Chapter 1

The sun set over the distant river, spreading a warm flush over the green land, and at that moment of brightness all the creatures of earth, animal and human, stopped to watch. She watched too from her tower window, propped up in the small wooden chair. Always she had loved this hour. Distantly it seemed to her, she could hear the voices of angels singing low. She often heard them now, in her great age. They sounded like the birds, whose sweet voices rang in the sky overhead as they flew south for the winter. She had always loved birds. Even as a child she would wait and watch for the first bird of spring and rejoice when it came. Her mother had told her about that, long ago, before the weariness of bearing ten children in as many years had destroyed the once-strong body. She had never forgotten what her mother had told her, even through all that had come after.

Her first memory was of the flowers, the flowers that grew in her mother's little garden in the castle courtyard. Even with all of her other chores, her mother had always found the time on warm days to tend her garden. Her mother, Marguerite, Lady Bonel, was French-born, slim and lovely, with waist length waving hair the color of walnuts that she covered, as married women should, with a wimple. She was strong then, and full of energy, and she would bring her baby daughter along with her to play in the dirt, her first born, Jacqueline, who had been named after her beloved French grandmother. The child had played in the dirt and watched the flowers grow, and learned the value and the beauty of living things. When the birds came, her mother never shooed them away, but instead scattered seeds for them, and spoke softly so they would not fear. In these early days in the little garden the bond between mother and daughter grew strong and unbreakable.

It was different with Jacqueline's father. That is not to say that he was a cold or unkind man, for he was not. Jacqueline could remember many moments of her early childhood when he would pick her up and swing her, and she would laugh with glee, or when he held her on his knee and told her a story to calm her fear of the thunderstorm that raged outside. She had loved her father. When more children came his attention was divided, as it was by the running of his great estate. But Jacqueline had still felt his love. Now, in her older years, when age and wisdom should have softened the harshness of memory, the remembrance of the child's father was colored by the memory of what he had become to her later. If she regretted one thing in her present life, it was that those beautiful childhood memories were shadowed by what had happened since. If only she could go back! But no, she had vowed long ago never to think of that. Time was an enigma, but the one certain thing about time was that it did not turn back, only moved inevitably forward. She put the wish from her mind and dozed as the room darkened.

"Sister. Sister!"

She opened her eyes to see the candle flame of the young novice who cared for her. "Sister Bernadette. I was dreaming."

"You," the young woman chided kindly. "You have always been a dreamer."

Sister Bernadette was practical and knew little of dreams. She got down to business, helping the old nun from the chair to the narrow wooden cot. "A chair was not made for sleeping," she scolded. "God invented cots for that purpose!"

"Oh, sister," the old nun chuckled softly. She thought to herself, *This young woman sees me as very old, no longer clear in my thinking. True, my mind drifts often- but oh, the thoughts come crystal clear.*

But she submitted to the young nun's will, was led to bed, and fell asleep again to the sound of the young nun singing softly.

Chapter 2

When had their happy lives begun to change? Was it the day her young brother died?

After Jacqueline, a son was born to the Bonels, and the next year, another son. Then came twin girls. A year after that came another son. All the children thrived, and the family rejoiced, for children were not always wont to thrive in those days. Lady Bonel was but twenty-two then, strong and healthy, and she bore healthy children. She delighted in her sons, Antoine, Louis, and Robert, though no less in her daughters, Jacqueline, and the twins, Marie and Joan.

Jacqueline was six when it happened. The memory of that day cut into her brain like the edge of a sharp sword. Robert had been beloved to her, a charming boy, with dark straight hair and rosy cheeks. She used to show him the birds in the garden, calling them by name, and he would listen, his round dark eyes glistening in wonder.

That day their father, Lord Bonel, and some of his men, were going hunting. It was a crisp day, near September's end. The children, clustered in the great hall near the fire, could hear the restless horse's neighs and the shouts of the men, betraying eagerness to be on their way. Robert was two. He had been playing quietly, rolling a bright ball back and forth, humming to himself as he often did. He had been there with his brother and sisters, their mother, and their nurse. Then he was not there.

They did not miss him immediately. When Lady Bonel noticed his absence, she did not panic, thinking that he had only wandered to the other side of the hall. And yet her voice, ringing in the huge dank room had a chilling quality, as if the voice knew somehow that all was not well, before the woman's mind grasped the truth.

"Robert!" To the child Jacqueline her mother's voice had a fearsome sound that day.

"Robert!"

The voice bounced back, echoing from the far wall. There was no other answer.

"Oh my God." This time their mother's voice was like a prayer. Lady Bonel rose and the young nurse with her.

"Watch the children, Yvonne." The calm of her voice was deadly. Yvonne, the nurse, put an arm around each of the twin's shoulders and watched Lady Bonel walk from the great hall. The walls echoed with her steps, pounding loudly in Jacqueline's ears. Just as her mother reached the door Jacqueline shrieked, "Mama!" and ran after her.

The old nun shook her head. This was painful, so painful. God's will. Had she ever really believed that? It was blasphemy to doubt. But what sort of God would strike down a sweet child with so vicious a blow? Jacqueline had questioned for a long time. Now in her old age she was more able to accept. But the pain and doubt had shadowed her childhood. Yet if she had never questioned, would she have become what she was now? It was too late to wonder.

Her mother had told her to go back to Yvonne. Perhaps for the first time Jacqueline defied her mother, showing the strength of will that would become more evident later.

"No! I'm coming with you!"

Why did Mama let me go with her that day? She had often wondered. Perhaps something in the mother was too wounded to care. For Lady Bonel had known. She had known, as she walked out of the courtyard, outside the castle gate, that no rosy-cheeked living boy would greet her with his smile. *Mama knew*, thought the old nun, *but she let me come anyway.*

They found him not far from the castle gate. He was crushed. Horse's hooves had trampled him almost beyond recognition. Never would she forget- at first, something red on the ground, like a tattered piece of cloth... what she had seen was her brother's blood, flowing red from his body, still warm. Jacqueline had screamed until her voice would no longer emerge from her throat. But the mother had not screamed. She knelt before what had so recently been her living son. She knelt for a long time. Then she had turned, taking her trembling daughter by the hand.

"We must get help," she said, in an everyday voice, calm and sure. "We must send someone for your father."

Jacqueline had been put to bed. Dimly she recalled the stifled shrieks and wails from the household. She recalled her father's face as she had never before seen it, shadowed, as though some devil held a black lowering cloud over his head. But the time passed. Her mother became full again with child. Her brother and sisters, having been spared the sight she had seen, forgot, as children will. No one ever knew how Robert had gotten out that day. Playfully, drawn by the horses, which he loved, and the excitement of the men, he must have crept outside unnoticed, and through the open gates. The men, galloping cheerfully out of the courtyard toward the woods, never saw him, never knew what the galloping hooves had left behind. They sorrowed too. Then they too forgot. But Jacqueline, her mother, and her father never forgot. There would always be a before and an after in Jacqueline's young life, with Robert at the center point.

She no longer thought of her brother often, and yet, thought of him was always with her. He did not often come to her conscious mind as he had been. He was more like a symbol, she came to see later, a symbol of purity, beauty, and innocent childhood that Jacqueline had lost that day. The tears had flowed and flowed until they ran dry. She did not recall ever crying again, unless it was for joy. She never cried again in sorrow, for there is no sorrow deeper than the loss of innocence.

Chapter 3

Her mother's next child was a boy, a boy they were afraid to love, for
fear such pain might come again. And fear was justified, for this baby was
sickly, and lived only to the age of three months. There were no tears at
his burial. They laid young Charles by the side of the brother he had never
known. It became easier this time to forget.

These incidents in Jacqueline's childhood stood out stark and clear,
though most memories of her early life the daily tasks, the comings and
goings of castle life, blended into each other, making the years merge.
But there were other things that she remembered, unevaluated memories,
colorful, like vivid dreams in which only the outline can be recalled.

Chapter 4

"Mother Alfreda is very ill, Sister," someone whispered in her ear. She shook her head, to push away the bitter dream. Her eyes opened and the form of a nun hovered before her, holding a candle. "Sister?"

It was no dream. The time had come.

Oh, Mother, she thought in anguish, and it was as though her own mother lay dying once again. That had been long ago. But she remembered…..

Jacqueline was twelve.

Her mother was pregnant again, with her tenth child. Seven of the children she had borne were still living. Jacqueline was helping to keep her younger brothers and sisters away from the birthing room. She played games with them, tried to get them to sing, but the children's voices could not drown out the sound of the mother's screams.

Jacqueline closed her eyes in horror, trying to push away the fearsome picture of her calm, lovely mother tortured, writhing and screaming in pain. So this is what happened to married women in the end. She could not bear to hear the screams of her beloved mother, to know that such pain was the result of bringing forth new life.

The moment came that awful day when Yvonne, who had been attending Lady Bonel for the birth, came running to the nursery.

"Children!" she cried, her eyes wild. "Come! Come see your dear mother." And the tender-hearted woman had burst into tears as she turned to flee back to the birthing room.

As calmly as they could the older girls, Jacqueline, Marie, and Joan, gathered the younger children together and followed Yvonne. The smell pierced their senses outside the heavy door, the smell of birth- and of death. They entered.

"Mama!" young Ralf cried, staring at the still figure on the bed.

'She is dead,' thought Jacqueline. But Lady Bonel stirred, inclined her head weakly toward her children, and said, "Come here," in a hoarse whisper.

Louis ran forward, followed by Ralf and Cecile, the younger children. The eleven-year-old Antoine moved stiffly toward his mother. The older girls moved nearer their mother's bed.

"I love you, my dears," Lady Bonel whispered, forcing the words out, then gasping for breath. She held out her hands to her three oldest daughters.

"Care for the little ones," she said. Her eyes closed.

"Mama!" Marie and Joan cried in one voice. Antoine wiped a tear from his cheek, and the little ones clamored. Lady Bonel's eyes flickered open again, looked beyond them. Her eyes met Jacqueline's.

"You…" she said, "Someday…" She could say no more, but her look was full of compassion. The look burned deep into Jacqueline's soul. She knew that her mother, standing on the edge between life and death, could see what they, the living, could not.

"Mama." Her voice, out of all the children's, was calm, but the pain of impending loss had made her numb.

Their father entered then. He ignored his children, going straight to his wife. He took her hand. On his face was a look of mingled pain and tenderness that Jacqueline had never seen before. He really loves her, she thought. An overwhelming sadness came over her. She turned and fled, and did not stop running until she reached a small nook in the castle wall where as a young child she sometimes had liked to take shelter. Even then she did not cry. She sat in her nook on a small ledge of rock and tried to clear her mind of all thought. She was not with her mother when the weary eyes at last closed. Two days later they buried the premature baby with the mother it had killed.

And now, Mother Alfreda! How many mothers can I lose in just one lifetime? the old nun thought with passion. "I shall go to her," she said to the nun who had brought the news. "Please help me." With effort, she pulled herself out of her straight wooden chair and they made their way slowly to the chamber of the Abbess.

The old nun's mind wandered. Mother Alfreda had come to England from France as a young girl, though she never explained the circumstances of her leaving her home. *She was not much older than me when I met her,* the old nun thought, *and yet her eyes already had the purity of a saint's. She saved me when I was fearful, when I almost lost faith again. She helped me become what I am now, to my great joy. It was after…after the horror…*

"Welcome, child," the young novice had said. Jacqueline looked closely into her face. "She is not much older than me," she thought. "But she is right. I am a child."

"We are glad that you have come." It had hurt to hear the kindness in that deep, rich voice, to see the compassion in those large, dark eyes beneath the wimple of a novice. Jacqueline had faltered, become fearful again.

"I cannot," she had said. "I…I should not enter a holy place."

"But we are all holy in the eyes of God. He will forgive you your sins. No," the young novice smiled, and the dim room became lighter. "He has forgiven you already."

So Jacqueline had entered, and in the peace of the place she had forged her way…

The novice was Mother Alfreda.

They reached the room. The memory of her own mother's death rushed back, and the old nun swayed, expecting the same acrid smell, but there was only the damp odor of stone walls. She knocked and entered. Shaking off the hands of the young novice who guided her, she slowly, deliberately, made her way to Mother Alfreda's bedside alone.

"Sister," Mother Alfreda said, her voice surprisingly clear. The eyes were still large and brilliant, the skin soft, gently unwrinkled, translucent, as though her gentle spirit made it glow. "I was waiting for you. Now I can rest."

"Oh, Mother." The old nun could hardly speak. She had not cried for most of her lifetime, yet now, to her horror, tears burned her dimmed eyes.

"Sister! I am surprised!" Mother Alfreda's voice, strong and sure, broke into the room. "Do you mourn? But I am moving forward. I am moving to a new life! Please," she laid her hand on the old nun's, "I do not fear." She laughed softly. "I am certain that we both protested at being born, for it was beyond our understanding. And yet how glad I am that I had this life! This we do not understand either. But my dear-could it be any less than this life has been?"

The old nun's eyes were clear now. "You are right, Mother Alfreda. And I am keeping you from your journey." She bent to kiss the beloved face, and whispered, "I wish you beauty on your way." Their eyes met. Then the old nun turned, walked steadily from the room, her back no longer bent. Mother Alfreda's eyes closed. Again Jacqueline was not there to see.

Chapter 5

The church was a very integral part of her early life, but at first it was a mindless, comforting part. She would go to mass with her family and her mind would drift away, as if in a dream, a gentle warming dream that left her at peace. Especially when she was older, after losing her mother, she would look to the church for comfort. The sonorous sound of the words, the beauty of the hymns, eased her mind. But that was all.

The inner connection came, but it did not happen in a church.

It was a day in early summer, a day Jacqueline's family had looked forward to, for special guests were visiting, brothers of Lord Bonel's. He seemed happier than he had been in years, and the whole household was affected by his mood. On that day they were all to go hunting, and to a picnic in the woods. All were excited. But Jacqueline, though she was pleased at her father's gladness, and liked these relatives very much, was not so pleased. She was tender-hearted, and disliked the heated ride of the hunt, the raucous cries of the trained falcons, and the blood of the poor victims. So she, along with two of her cousins, and the younger children, detached themselves from the main party, agreeing to meet later for the meal.

As they rode slowly through the woods, Jacqueline talked for awhile with her two cousins, who were near her age, and pleasing, intelligent girls. Then the children, who were riding just behind, clamored for a rest. Yvonne, who had come to tend the children, called for a stop.

"I shall ride on a bit," Jacqueline said, and no one protested. She enjoyed the company of her cousins, but on a day as beautiful as this one she wanted to be alone for awhile, to hear the sounds of the breeze and the bird's song. Her horse, Padgett, plodded on slowly, and she fell into an almost trance-like state, mesmerized by the gentle clip-clop of the hooves.

They came upon a running stream, and stopped to rest and drink. After sipping the cool clear water from her hands, Jacqueline leaned back against a tree while Padgett grazed, and looked around her.

The green glade stretched out all around. The tree trunks were straight and tall, with the leaves growing near the top, giving shade from the vivid sun. Dark moss carpeted the ground. The rippling noise of the stream, the whisper of the wind in the leaves, were conducive to deep thought. Jacqueline began to ponder, as she often did, what her place in the world was to be. Since her mother's passing Jacqueline, as the eldest, had taken her place in supervising the household. Though she had been young at the time, she had been apprenticed to her mother as a child, and knew much of household management already. What she did not know, she was able to learn quickly, with the aid of servants who had long served Lord Bonel. Because there was no lady of the house, Jacqueline had not been sent to another noble household for her education, as many young noblewomen were. She and her sisters, Marie and Joan, had been educated in their own household, as they took over the tasks of overseeing the spinning, cleaning, the storage of food, meal preparation, and other domestic chores which had become second nature to all of them. Now Jacqueline was sixteen, of an age to marry. What did marriage mean but more of the same? Supervising another man's household. And perhaps, bearing his children. Remembering how her mother had died, Jacqueline could not help but fear.

And was there not more to life? Was there not more?

The question seemed to hang heavy in the air, so strangely that for a moment Jacqueline wondered if she had spoken it aloud. She looked up. Through the lace of leaves she saw that a cloud had blocked the sun; then as she gazed, it broke apart, and the sun touched golden fingertips to the earth in a blaze of yellow light. The clouds rolled and billowed, like a stormy ocean, and the blue behind was like a gem. A sense of bonding with that blazing natural spectacle made Jacqueline throw out her arms toward it, then, in an excess of joy and wonder that made her catch her breath, then embrace herself.

As quickly as it came, it faded. The clouds became quiet and the sun resumed its natural appearance in the sky. But Jacqueline was changed.

What happened that day? thought the old nun. Even in the wisdom that old age had brought, she did not really know. Did it make a difference in her life? Nothing had seemed to change. And yet, for Jacqueline, it was as though time had stopped for one brief moment, and the world had given her one of its deepest secrets.

She sat for a long time, watching the sky, her heart pounding, the air around her filled with a strange electricity. But no further sign was given. Finally she mounted Padgett and rode away. She pondered what she had seen, telling no one. The spectacle had been so dazzling, so beautiful and unearthly, that she half suspected others to remark on it. But no one did. No one ever did. She began to think it had truly been a sign, meant for her eyes alone. She prayed fervently, "God, I do not know what you want of me. But you want me to be more than I now am, I know!"

That night, after the riot of the picnic, Jacqueline lay sleepless on her pallet. She prayed again that she might understand the strange spectacle in the woods. And a slow realization came to her that she could not marry. For some reason God had chosen her for some other task. *Is this what my mother saw for me on her last day?* She wondered. *And did she see such beauty as I saw?* Jacqueline clung to the thought. Dying, there is a moment when the person hovers on the brink of life, and time, past, present, future, has no meaning. Time is interconnected, forever is compacted into one moment. *I stood on the brink between life and death, she thought, and I saw even though I am fully alive. I saw. Why?*

At first she questioned continually, sensing within herself some great meaning in what she had seen, and in the fact that she had such an experience. At the spinning of cloth, in the midst of overseeing the preparation of a meal, she would stop and wonder, *Why? What did it mean?* Perhaps she was not humble enough, perhaps she was deluding herself. Had God chosen her? And for what?

The answer came, but it did not come through conscious thought. Logic could not discover the answer, for God's reasons were not based on the logic of a merely human mind. It was when she stopped questioning so fiercely, when she prayed humbly, "Let me know what I must do," then put it from her mind, that the answer came. It came so gently she hardly knew it had come. When she realized, her soul was at peace, and she knew what she must do.

Her work finished for the day, Jacqueline had gone for a walk in the fields outside the castle walls. It was still August, but the day was cool and breezy, though full of sunshine, and the wind swirled her heavy skirts and blew her dark hair from beneath her shawl. She yanked at the shawl that all proper ladies must wear off her head and felt a delicious freedom as the long shining strands of her hair blew free, down across her face, swirling around her shoulders. Her one vanity was her hair, and if she could claim one beauty, it was that. She ran her hands through the silky stuff, then began to run. The tall grass caught her feet in its tangles, making her stumble, but she only laughed, and kept running until she could no longer.

How clear my mind was that day! the old nun thought. *I don't believe I ever knew such a moment of joy and freedom at any other time. How well I remember. I asked nothing, questioned nothing- and the answer came.*

Jacqueline had at last stopped to rest, sinking down on a mat of soft grass. All around her the field stretched, filled with white and yellow flowers. To her left the field curved down and below, in a gentle valley, were the woods in which the vision had come to her. From her vantage point on the hill she could see far beyond these green fields, fruitful with late summer. Some spare fluffy clouds floated low on the horizon, flushed pink with the lowering sun.

She sat for a time, watching. The sun moved lower still, and the sky's flush grew deeper, until it was a spreading fire across the western horizon. Then the rim of the setting sun blazed in one brief flash before it sank below the distant hills. Filled with emotion, Jacqueline rose, knowing what she had not known when she had come. The vision in the woods had truly been a sign. She had been chosen. Her experience in the woods that day had been immersed in meaning. No matter what else happened in her life, she had had one moment of communication with God when she and the universe were one, when her soul, for one brief instant in time, had been lifted above and beyond herself, and left her changed. With new, certain faith she started down the hill toward the castle gates.

She would become a nun.

Chapter 6

In those days, many women who entered holy orders did not do so out of free choice. Fathers with many daughters to marry off and provide dowries for would send the youngest to a convent. Jacqueline's father, as she well knew, planned for his daughters to marry. Marriage was the best way to create lasting bonds between neighboring families. Lord Bonel had enough wealth to provide each of his daughters with a goodly dowry. He wanted to see them married. And for his eldest daughter the time was already becoming late.

But the worst of it, Jacqueline knew, was that slowly, over the years, Lord Bonel had developed a bitterness against the church. With the tragic death of his second born son the rage had begun, rage at a God who would allow such a thing to happen. The bitterness grew as the gentle Lady Bonel took her final breath. Jacqueline had seen how well her father loved her mother and she had pondered, although the idea was disturbing, whether he blamed himself. Lady Bonel had died, after all trying to give birth to his son. Many women died in childbirth, but most women were not so loved by their husbands as her mother had been. Jacqueline sensed the bitterness in her father more than she could see or hear it. He went to mass, just as before, he prayed, and said no harsh word against the priests. He did not blaspheme and took the sacraments. But his heart was not in these things that he did. He did them and walked out of the chapel with the same hard and bitter sadness deep within him. Jacqueline saw this. She knew the church had not comforted her father in his terrible need. This, she knew, would make him fight her desire. He would not want to give his first-born to the church. He wanted to see her married, with children around her. Children…like her mother had had children….

The old nun's eyes shut for a moment, as if the pain of memory was too hard to bear. *I got what I desired in the end,* she thought. *But what a price I paid. A terrible price…*

Jacqueline had bided her time, knowing she must. She went to mass and prayed, and kept her secret in her heart. She walked in the woods and fields, glorying in the beauty of God's earth. As time went on the burden of waiting became painful. In dark moments when sleep would not come, the shadows of doubt would creep softly into her mind. She shook them off. Later, after she had found her dream and entered the convent, the doubts so prevalent inside her would make her more intense in her religious duties. She had wanted to stifle all doubt, all questions, and be wholly pure. Now, in her great age, she let the questions flow freely. It was only human to question; it did no harm. She knew now that doubts were building blocks to something better. The church had been created when Christ was alive, but human thought had molded it throughout the centuries. She loved the growing and floundering as well as the strength and certainty. In her youth, she had needed the church's strength. She had drawn on its sameness, its steadiness, and the power of her conviction of where she belonged had helped her to wait.

She waited for many weeks. All during that time the immensity of the desire grew. Then one day in the fall the subject of marriage came up. It was Joan who mentioned it, speaking casually as the women went about their sewing for the winter. Though her words were casual, they made a frozen lump of Jacqueline's heart.

"Do you know that young man, Sir Andrew Morse, Jacqueline?"

"I am not sure, who is he?" she had replied, unsuspecting.

A smile played on Joan's lips. She glanced at her twin, Marie, who answered for her.

"His family lives in London, but he has come here often of late to speak to Father. You have seen him. He is a handsome man, in his thirties, a knight. He has dark curly hair and sturdy features and he speaks like a gentleman. I know you have seen him."

"I suppose so. I have not paid much attention."

"You should, Jacqueline," Joan said. "I heard him and Father talking." She leaned closer, lowered her voice so the servants working nearby would not hear. "The 'business' they are discussing is you!"

It took a moment for Joan's words to sink in. When she realized their import, Jacqueline looked at her sister in horror, her quickly moving fingers on the fabric stilled.

"Aren't you excited? Do you know what this means? Soon we will have husbands too, Lina!" Marie, in her gladness, called her older sister by a pet name of her childhood, when she and her twin could not say 'Jacqueline'.

Jacqueline looked at each of them, seeing the happiness in their eyes. She did not want to spoil it-oh, no, she loved her sisters! But they would soon know anyway. It was best.

She laid down her needle and cloth and looked into Joan's eyes, then Marie's.

"Sisters," she had said. She remembered every word in crystal clear memory, even now. "Sisters." Her voice hung strangely in the suddenly chill air, like a sound coming from far away.

"I cannot marry him. I cannot." It was an effort to push the words past the enormous heaviness in her throat. Marie and Joan stared at her in disbelief.

"But why, Jacqueline?" Marie said in amazement. "He is a good man, and he has some wealth. You would live very comfortably. Do you think... did you hear something about him? Perhaps something Father doesn't know?"

"Oh, no," Jacqueline interrupted. "It is not like that." She inhaled deeply, as if trying to draw support from the very air. "I want to enter the convent." The words, after all, were not so very hard to say. They had been spoken, clear and sure, and they left a ringing behind them on the air.

Jacqueline found strength now. "I have wanted this for a long time, more than anything. I have not told Father; perhaps I have waited too long. But I must stop his plans. Will you help me? Will you support my wishes?"

"Jacqueline, I am puzzled," Joan stared at her squarely. "You in the church? It never occurred to me."

"No, perhaps not," Jacqueline chose her words carefully. "It is not easy to explain. I have... been called, in a sense. God wants me, I think, for something. I am to serve him somehow in this world."

"Lina," Marie said somewhat timidly, "I do not want to question you but-well, you have not seemed so terribly pious. I mean- oh, you have been good, you are a good person, but you have shown no great love for the church, no more than any of us, who do not want that type of life. I do not mean to hurt you," she added quickly.

Jacqueline smiled. Talking to her sisters about her desire after keeping it bottled up inside her for so long was only serving to strengthen her faith.

"No, Marie, your questions do not hurt me," she said. "But I do love the church, and I love God. There are many ways to show that love. I find God in many things, not only in church." As she spoke, her face grew joyous. "God is not only in church, but everywhere! In the birds that sing, in the woods and fields. God is in people too. I have felt him to be within me." She finished, clasping her hands together in fervor. "It is right," she said quietly.

Her sisters were silent for a moment. Then Joan said, "I see that it has to be. I am glad for you, Jacqueline." Marie said, "We will help you."

My dear sisters, the old nun thought. *If I knew then, if I only knew that my very desire would cause me to be forever parted from them! But if I had known, would I have done differently? No. I would have done the same. I had to.*

Her sisters helped her plan how to approach their father and even offered to confront him with her, but in the end she decided to do it alone. She took him aside one day, after he had his fill of a particularly good meal, and said that she must speak to him. He was in a good mood, having had a good hunt that day, which he greatly enjoyed. Jacqueline hoped that his mood would carry over even after he had heard her plans. The hope was short-lived.

I still tremble in fear when I remember, the old nun thought, *even though it was so long ago, almost a lifetime ago.* She shut her eyes tight against the memory. *I had prepared myself, or so I thought, for his anger. What I had not expected was his rage, that irrational rage. I had no weapons in the face of his rage.*

"Father," she had begun. She had practiced her speech with Marie and Joan. "I love you very much, and I want to please you. But I cannot marry Andrew Morse."

He had looked startled and said, "Jacqueline, how did you know?" He smiled. "But why can you not marry Sir Morse? Is there another man who has caught your eye? I never suspected..." His voice was merry; it was obvious that he was pleased with the idea that his eldest daughter had begun to notice men. She could not bear that he thought this.

"Oh, no, Father! Please listen. I want to do as you say, Father, I want to please you- but what I want more than anything in the world is to become a nun!"

He stared at her as though stricken. His face grew red with rage. He reached up his hand and slapped her. The blow was so unexpected, so cruel, that Jacqueline said nothing, did nothing. She merely stood and stared at her father as her fair cheek stung red from the blow.

"Never," her father breathed. The low cruel tone was more frightening than a shout could ever be. "Do not ever speak of this to me again. I will see you married. Now go!"

She had turned away, filled with a crushing pain, and walked slowly from the room. She did as he wished- she never mentioned her desire again. The desire was as strong as ever. She would be a nun. But if her father would not give her his blessing she would have to defy him.

Despite my conviction, I was so full of pain, the old nun thought. *I loved my father, longed to do as he pleased. But he denied my deepest wishes. I could never quite love him in the same way after that day. And why did he feel the way he did? Did he have so much bitterness against the church, against God?*

It had taken her a long time, and much pondering, to understand. Her father was bitter. In his heart he had turned against God. But his anger arose from his daughter's defiance. He needed that power over his children. Most of all, he felt responsible for her fear of marriage. How long it had taken her to learn this! He knew she had watched her mother die giving birth to his son. He knew that she was old enough to remember, and to fear the same thing for herself. His rage at her request had been partially for himself.

But I am the one who felt his rage, the old nun thought. *I carried it with me inside. The one thing he did not know, and could not understand, was that I wanted to enter the convent out of love and conviction, not fear.* She sighed heavily. The air in the small room smelled musty and old, as old as herself. Soon a young novice would come to wake her for Matins, help her to the chapel and back again after. How painful it was to no longer have control over one's own flesh! It kept her bound to earth, dependent on younger, stronger bodies to set her old bones in motion. *My mind commands,* she thought, *but my body does not obey.* She stared into the black darkness of the room. That had happened once before, when she had still been young. Just after her father's bitter rage and rejection of her dream.....

Chapter 7

The marriage plans with Sir Andrew Morse had fallen through and though Jacqueline never learned why, she thanked God for having at least given her that extra time. She had warned her sisters not to speak on her behalf to their father. "He will only hate you too."

"He does not hate you, Jacqueline!" Marie had cried passionately. But Jacqueline knew that if he hated that deepest desire, her innermost passion, then truly he did hate the person she was.

In his anger, Lord Bonel did not wait long to begin laying new marriage plans with a family that owned a vast neighboring estate. He spoke to Jacqueline harshly about the matter, saying that he expected her obedience. She began to feel trapped and desperate.

So why did I do what I did? She had wondered many times, years later. *I was so against marriage and all that it meant- how could it have happened? Was it because my father had turned so cold? Was it because my brothers made bawdy jokes about my husband to be and I could turn to no man in my family for support? Or was it perhaps that if a choice had to be made, I would be the one to make it?*

By that time she had been eighteen, already overripe for marriage in a time when many girls married at age thirteen, or even younger. In the years after her mother's death there had been such a gap in her father's life that he had done as little as it was possible for him to do. He had traveled much, gone hunting, his favorite pastime, and tried to bury his sorrow in these pleasures, with little thought for work. His older daughters and sons managed as best they could, and with the help of a few trusted men who had long been vassals of Lord Bonel, they had run the estate. Lord Bonel had shown no signs of seeking a wife for himself, as many men did after losing their first wives. Gradually, Lord Bonel had resumed his duties, and under his skilled rule the estate flourished. He could afford to provide his daughters with healthy dowries and bargain for marriage with the best men. Men whom, to Jacqueline, seemed hard and cold, like her father, concerned with buying a wife as they would buy sheep. They cared nothing for her true desires.

So when had she first seen him?

Moving about his duties as a stable boy, most likely, never really noticing the thin quick form as he rubbed down and fed the horses after a long day's ride. Jacqueline did not ride often, being busy with the running of the household, and so she had seen him little, though he had worked for Lord Bonel for many years, starting when he was only a scruffy peasant boy.

But he had grown tall, and his cheeks were shadowed with a mature fuzz, and his tangled light brown hair hung to his chin. He had gotten the horses ready for Jacqueline, her sisters, and the servants who were to accompany them, one day when they were to ride into town to market. They were dressed in fine clothes, befitting their good birth, and talking excitedly, for they went into town only rarely, and it was a great treat. She should never have noticed him at all. But as he handed her the reins she happened to look at him and it seemed suddenly as though she were drowning in a deep green pool. He gazed at her intently, his eyes piercing hers, and it was she who looked away first. She tried to brush aside this incident, for she wanted to think of nothing that day; not the stable boy's gaze, not the bargaining for her marriage. But while she was successful at pushing aside her impending doom, she could not forget the stable boy's green eyes.

How I chastised myself for even thinking of him, the old nun remembered. *If I only knew what would come later! I would not have chastised myself for mere thought...*

She had, at long last, forgiven herself, as God, Brother Giles, and Sister Alfreda had forgiven her long ago. But it had taken her long years to forgive herself, to stop regretting. *And yet again, if I had known, would I have done differently?*

She had thought of him, and an image formed in her mind that was an entity in itself, an image of his form, angular and thin, shining with a light that seemed to emanate from his green eyes. His look had disturbed her; it was not a look that he, a lowly stable boy, should have given to her, the eldest daughter of a wealthy nobleman. But had had given it, and that created a bond between them, a tie thin as cobweb, but strong.

Two days after the trip to town she contrived to see him again, walking out to the stables on the pretense of seeing her horse, Padgett, after her daily chores were done. She had dressed carefully, in a dress that was plainly styled but a bright and flattering shade of blue. She wore a thin veil over her shining hair, pulling a few strands out from beneath it. As she walked toward the stables she felt a sting of conscience and self-doubt. What was it that she was doing? But she had to know why he had looked at her so piercingly, so knowingly. She felt, even while aware of its impossibility, that he knew of her desire to become a nun. How could he know? Only her father and sisters had been told. But deep inside, on a level beyond intellect, she felt his awareness of her inner being. She had to find out more about him.

When she walked into the stables, toward the stall where Padgett was kept, she was aware of his presence with all her senses. The awareness was like an entity standing sharply in the air between them. She knew that he had ceased his work; she felt him stop, rather than seeing it. There was a strange excitement running through her, a feeling that she did not understand, and rather feared. But even the fear that made her heart pound wildly was not unpleasant. *No!* she thought wildly, but she did not leave. She reached out to touch her horse's silky head, and he neighed softly. Then she turned to face the boy.

Those eyes! Long and heavy-lashed, again they drew her in. She was hardly aware of the rest of him; he was a creature of eyes, eyes that had hands to reach out and grasp. She looked away, feeling dazed, dreamlike. This encounter between her and the stable boy should not be happening at all. But it was. She consciously made herself aware of her station. She inclined her head toward him, without looking at his face.

"My horse seems well cared for." How banal were the words. Yet they were infused with meaning.

"I have been watching you," he said in a low voice, as if it were the most proper answer to her statement. She caught her breath. She had not expected him to say it so openly. Yet he had. She could not answer.

"I know it is not my place to say this. But I think- I think you are unlike the others."

He had caught her interest deeply. "In what way?" she asked, despite herself.

"There is something more inside you. You have thoughts- the kind of thoughts most do not have."

She was astounded at this truth. "Why do you think that?"

"I watch people. They think me stupid. I let them. It is convenient. But I am very well aware of things."

His words made her wonder how much he knew. She did not ask.

"I must go." She turned away even as she spoke, and fairly ran away from him. Feelings poured through her, overwhelming feelings, emotions she could not define. She would not let herself define them.

Later that night, lying on her pallet in the chamber she shared with her sisters, Jacqueline thought of him. *What is he doing? Does he sleep now? Why does he watch me?* The thoughts burned her brain. Her mouth felt dry and her heart beat much too fast.

But I am for God! she thought passionately. *I do not want a man, much less a boy who is not even yet a man!*

In the days that followed she threw herself into her work and after a long day's labor, sat with her sisters by the fire, sewing and talking. But thought of him arose, unbidden. She tried to bury his image, to cover it with dust, but his words, his blazing eyes, returned to haunt her.

She asked about him, surreptitiously, casually, making stray innocent remarks about him to the servants or to her father's men. One of them, a knight who, when he was not fighting, spent much time with his beloved horses, gave her information.

"Oh, Guillaume. A good lad. Mother was French. Lost her to the pox. He came here as a young boy of nine."

His mother was French, like her own dear mother! "Oh?" she had said, trying not to act as though the answer was important. "And how long ago was that?"

"Let me see- must be about eight years. He is seventeen now, my Lady."

Seventeen! A year younger than she. He could never be more to her than a servant. She must remember her place, both earthly and spiritual. Her earthly place was that of a well-born lady. And her spiritual place was to serve God as a nun. Yet, though she could not acknowledge it to herself, that burning desire had lessened in its immediacy. She wanted time, to think to decide... to decide what? What could this ever be to her? Surely she could not consider her father's stable boy as a husband! Yet in the back of her mind she knew she was no longer eager to leave for a convent so soon.

"Sister," a voice said gently, "we need your aid." She awoke dazedly, remembering him, the young boy of her early days, Guillaume of the green eyes....

"Yes," she said, her voice bleary with sleep. She was always ready to do her duty. She owed the convent so much. She owed it her life.

"Sister, Mother Matilda needs your help. The church roof is leaking and she fears it will become worse, but we have no money for repairs until the harvest. You have been here long, Sister. She wants to ask your advice."

"Of course. It has happened before, as I recall, when I was cellaress. I will be glad to speak with her of it."

Old. The old were called upon for odd reasons, then forgotten in the rush of dailiness, in the comings and goings of brisk young life.

But I will help, the old nun thought, as she awaited the abbess. In deference to her old age the new young abbess was coming to her. It seemed somewhat ironic. For so long after she had come to the convent, her sin had haunted her. She had given herself to the lowliest chores. Now in her great age, she held all the nuns' respect. She pitied the young, uncertain Jacqueline, pitied her, seeing her as a hurt child. But for a long time she had condemned her as a sinner, a harlot. She would never forget how she had been led to that sin. If indeed it had been a sin.

Jacqueline had made a conscious effort to forget Guillaume the stable boy, which had only served to implant his image more firmly in her mind. She began to wonder why he watched her, what he wanted of her, and the question of what God wanted seemed much less immediate. She chastised herself for her mind's wandering. *God is testing me,* she thought, *and I am miserably failing.*

But as she learned more about the boy, Guillaume, by listening to idle talk around the castle, by paying attention to servant's gossip, she began to wonder whether there was a more noble purpose in her confused feelings for this boy. He had had a hard life. His mother had died when he was young. His father had been slovenly, and sent him into the world at the age of nine to fend for himself. In her pity, a new light shone. Perhaps she was to show him goodness, to turn him on the path to God. She could show him a more gentle side to life. But how should she go about serving God in this new way?

She must talk to him of course. There was no other way to convey her message. She must talk to him where no one else could hear.

She planned carefully. Her opportunity came not long after. She chose a day when her father and his men were gone for the day, along with her brothers. After they had left, she had sent word to the stable that she wanted her horse prepared for riding that afternoon, and she wanted someone to accompany her.

Jacqueline did her work in a fever that morning, knowing full well that her plan would work. When the time came, she went out to the stables in excitement and anticipation. As she had thought, he was there, holding her horse by the reins.

"Thank you," she said as he handed Padgett over to her, trying to quell the nervous excitement in her voice. "Who is to accompany me? I sent word."

Was it her imagination that made her think his look was knowing? "There is no one here, Lady." His answer was that of a servant, but his eyes were bold. "No one but me."

Her plan had worked. "You will have to come then," she said. His eyes probed hers for a second more, then he took another horse and readied it. She mounted Padgett by herself and rode out of the castle gates at a trot. A moment later she heard his horse following.

Instinctively she headed toward the woods, but stopped upon reaching the fringe.

"I am tired," she said. She slipped off her horse before he could assist her and sank down into the deep soft grass. He dismounted too, and stood watching her.

"I wanted to tell you something," she said, looking past him, down into the green gold valley. He stirred, but did not speak. "Please sit down."

He sat, surveying her intently. She met his eyes.

"I want to tell you something," she repeated, feeling a little foolish. Her purpose did not seem so noble now. She was not certain how to begin.

"I know things about you. You have not had an easy life," she began, then hesitated. Somehow, sitting out in the grass at the border of the colored October forest, with the silver river below them, her words sounded false, unnatural. She tried again.

"Do you worship, Guillaume?" Her voice was almost a whisper.

He hesitated, then said, "You wish me to say yes."

"Only tell the truth! I want you to answer whatever is true."

"No. I do not worship."

"Why?"

"I …cannot say. I know I would be dubbed a heretic, but I do not think God watches over us. Perhaps he cares for the rich and able- people like your father. But he does not care for poor peasants like me."

"Guillaume, you are wrong." She was startled. She had not really expected such an answer, and now that she had it, she was not sure how to convey what she felt was God's love. *I am so lacking!* she thought. *I should be able to make God's love for this boy abundantly clear!*

"Guillaume. Perhaps you are in this position for a reason." She remembered her vision and a surge of faith rushed through her. "I was in the woods one day and I saw- oh, I cannot describe it. It was wondrous! I knew then that God loved me and wanted me for some special task…" She looked at him, feeling embarrassed. Had she really meant to tell him so much? How could this be? How could she be speaking her innermost experiences to her father's stable boy? He voiced her unspoken question.

"How is it that you tell me this, Lady?"

"I… I am not sure. I thought….I suppose I thought that it might help you. I do not know why I told you."

She looked down at her hands, which were twisting blades of grass sharply until they split.

"Perhaps we should go." She rose, reaching for the reins of her grazing horse.

"Let me help you!" Guillaume jumped to his feet, reaching for her horse, Their hands brushed. She felt a tingle in her fingers that ran through her whole body, and she pulled her hand sharply away. He had felt it too. For a moment they stood, uncertain of the next move. Then slowly, she mounted her horse by herself, and he mounted his. They rode in silence back to the castle.

Chapter 8

The months passed, bringing winter to the land. Time hung heavy on Jacqueline, hovered over her, whispered threats in her ear. She lived in a state of nervous excitement. Three things only seemed real. One was her own restless spirit, her desire to serve God. Only, she no longer felt utterly certain of what her path must be. The creature that was she was an entity in pain, a being of moods and feelings and desires that she could not decipher. She was an enigma to herself.

The second reality was her father's desire for her to marry. She feared it the more because he had not mentioned it for so long. Surely one day he would come to her and say, "I have found a husband for you. You are to be married in the spring." She had consulted her sisters, and even her brothers, but they knew nothing of their father's will. She could not approach her father. So she waited for the ax to fall.

The third, the sharpest, and yet the most elusive reality was Guillaume. It was almost as though Guillaume, the boy, did not exist, but Guillaume, the restless spirit that haunted her dreams was very much alive. She had not seen him since that day in early October. Now late November had frozen the ground, and she could not express a desire to go riding as an excuse to see him. So she waited. The pain of waiting fit itself to her like a suit of mail. She yearned for the lost brother who would have been her closest companion had he lived. She yearned to see the green-eyed stable boy again. But she had nobody but herself. Even her nook in the castle wall had long since crumbled.

Chapter 9

The old nun dozed, then awakened sharply. A vague fearful aura hung over the room, dissipating slowly. *A dream,* she thought, *only a dream.* But dreams were filled with the demons that wrench the soul. She could not sleep again that night. She must be awake to fight the demons with the power of God that was within her. *We are all alone in the final hours,* she thought. *And we are alone in the midst of the deep dark night when an unnamed terror settles upon us.*

A long time ago, when she had been young, the night had stirred far different feelings within her. She would never forget the night she had finally seen him again, after the long reprieve....

Jacqueline had been walking down the empty winding passageway to the castle kitchen. It was evening in mid-winter, and she was going to see to a late supper for her father, who had just returned from a journey.

Guillaume was there. At first she saw a shadowy figure, and she stopped short in fear. Then he stepped into the light of her candle, and the green eyes pierced her. An impetuous rush of emotion washed over her, making her sway. The candle in her hand flickered sharply.

He started, seeming as started as she. Then very slowly, in a moment that lasted an eternity, he walked toward her.

He stopped very close. Their breaths mingled in the damp chill air.

"Where are you going?" His voice was low, and soft as a caress.

"To the kitchens." Did he hear her blood pounding? "How do you come to be here?"

"I come when it gets too cold in the stables. There is a way...." His voice drifted into silence. *He feels it too,* she thought wildly. *He knows I want him....* She had never acknowledged it to herself, but as he stood before her, so close, yet not touching, she wanted him and her chest was tight with the painful and unfamiliar emotion. Then she came to herself, forcing awareness.

"I must go. I must see to my father's supper." She started past him.

"Wait!" His voice rang out, echoing against the far wall. There was a yearning in it that she did not want to hear.

"Jacqueline..."

It was the first time he had ever spoken her name. The word seemed to freeze in the air and materialize, an entity unto itself.

"I must go." She squeezed her eyes shut to stay the tears, bit her tongue to kill the bitter inner pain. She hurried toward the kitchens.

Later that night, in her pallet in the chamber she shared with her sisters, strange fires stirred within her, and his vague and burning image floated in her half-waking dreams.

Chapter 10

Moments come, pass, and are gone, the old nun thought, *but the memories burn themselves into our minds forever. Some memories are shades of grey, made dull by the many long years. Some are in vivid color, hallucinatory, tangible. I have too many memories. I live immersed in them now. The life is drifting from my body. I wait here, in this bare room, and my life is but a prelude to the grave.*

Somehow, the thought was not a saddening one. It was more like a glimpse of the freedom to come.

She gazed out of the narrow window. Far in the distance a jagged lightning bolt stung the sky, followed by a roll of thunder. *Storms are as full of beauty as the gentle rain, or the sunset,* she thought, in a wonder that filled her with a mercurial joy. The storm rose from behind the hills, filling the whole surrounding earth with its majestic force. The walls of her tower room trembled. She sat quietly, her inner tremors stilled. She sat calmly, open to the violence of the storm. *This too is God's creation.* That thought had never struck so deeply before.

Then the storm passed and the world lay still, as though newborn. The mists rose over the hills, wafting about like the ghosts of those who inhabited the land long ago. A breeze blew in through the narrow window, rustling her veil. She felt the peace of nature descend upon her. Strange, how nature had always brought her peace, while people had not. Though she had loved her family desperately, in the end they brought her pain because of that love.

And loving that tall, young, green-eyed boy- what had that brought? To think of it, the gall rose to her throat. It had been hard for her to forgive that. Even now…she had prayed long and hard that God may help her forgive. But had she? *I must, before I die,* she thought. *That is one thing in my life I have yet to do. Forgive my father.*

She turned away from the bitter thoughts, to the open window. The breeze washed over her like a gentle birdsong, washing her mind clear. As she watched, a small sparrow winged its way to her window and settled on the sill. She stayed very still. The bird fluffed its feathers and picked them clean. Then, sensing no danger, it settled down to rest. She breathed softly, not moving in her chair, loving the closeness of the trusting bird, remembering her mother, whom the birds had loved. It stayed awhile, then, called by some force beyond human knowledge, it spread its wings and soared out into the darkening world.

The old nun sat in wonder and gratitude as the in-blowing breeze grew colder and the world faded into night.

Chapter 11

There were mutterings in the castle toward winter's end, muttering that grew into cries of fear. It started with the small child of one of the serving women. He had grown ill and had to be sent to bed. "Just a small fever," said his mother, though her brow was wrinkled with worry. The next day the child was dead. But his mother never knew, for she too was delirious with fever. The pox, the dreaded pox, had come in with winter's frosty hands, sweating the body and chilling the heart until it stilled.

Knowledge struck terror into everyone's hearts. There was nothing to be done. All who lived in the castle may have been exposed to the swiftly moving disease. Only a few gathered their belongings and fled. Most stayed; they had nowhere else to go. The healthy nursed the sick, waiting for their turns. Some, miraculously, recovered. Some lived, but with the dreaded ugly scars remaining on their skin to tell the tale. Others were not so lucky.

Jacqueline and her family escaped the first round of the pox, though daily they heard word of their beloved servants and friends falling ill. The children had been cloistered in a suite of upstairs rooms to protect them from exposure. Many people reverted to the ancient beliefs, making amulets, chanting rhythmic songs. All prayed to God for the wretched disease to ease its ravages, while bowing to God's will when a precious life was taken.

Jacqueline and her siblings did their work as well as possible in the strange hush of the usually bustling household. They heard the moans and wails for the sick and dying. They worked silently, in fear, in pain for their friends. *Such is life,* thought Jacqueline. *We must know the evil along with the good.*

Beneath the horror of all that was happening she thought of Guillaume. At first she thought only of the meeting in the castle passageway, and the meaning of it, and wondered whether he thought of her. Something had changed that day, had increased the current of emotion between them. When it occurred to her that he could have fallen ill, the thought struck her suddenly, like a piercing arrow. Her heart began to beat so swiftly that she felt she would choke. She clasped her hand to her throat in an effort to calm her breathing and tried to think. How could she find out? How could she know whether he was ill….whether he was alive? Or if he had the pox, and lived, had it ravaged those firm and beloved features?

But she must still her fears until nightfall. Then she would creep from the cloistered rooms, out to the stables, and see for herself. There was nothing else she could do.

She was very quiet and still for the next few hours, her breath coming in quick rasping gasps, waiting, waiting. No one noticed her trepidation, wrapped in cocoons of fear as they were. Night fell. Someone brought them a hasty mean of bread and porridge, and thin wine. They ate in silence, then she and Joan and Marie put the young Ralf and Cecile to bed. The other boys, Antoine and Louis, being older, were staying with their father.

When the last restless sleeper was breathing slow and even, Jacqueline crept from the bed. None of them bothered to undress for bed in the winter, so she flung a cloak over her faded brown housedress and went to the door.

Quietly, not daring to breathe, she lifted the heavy bolt and pushed the door gently. It creaked. She gasped, then gazed toward the sleeping forms. No one stirred.

I remember those moments as if it had happened yesterday, the old nun thought. *Even now I still dream of sleepers and creaking doors- somehow there is always terror on the other side. I half expected to find something terrible when I reached the stables. I did not find what I expected. But in a way...was it not terrible after all?*

Somehow she had slipped out the door, leaving it ajar behind her. She ran down the stairs as if in a dream, paying no attention to her surroundings, her whole being focused on her destination.

The cold wrapped her in a fierce shawl when she stepped outside. Her heart pounded so hard she felt she could hear it in the silent night. She ran to the stables, slipping on the ice, picking herself up and running again. Her hood blew out behind her, her cloak billowed. She reached the stables, pushed open the door. At that moment it occurred to her that Guillaume, if he was here, might not be the only one sleeping in the stables. She stood quiet, consciously stilling her ragged breathing. In the dim light of the shining moon she made out the forms of the horses, their heads drooping in repose. A cat meowed softly. Nothing else stirred.

Guillaume! It seemed for a moment that she had called his name aloud, but she had not. She moved toward the hayloft where she thought he might sleep.

There was the low sound of breathing as she approached. Was it him? Was it him? She longed to run to him, grab him, shake him, cry, "You are alive!" Was it him?

She crept closer to the reclining form on the crude pallet in the hay. She made out a slender shape covered in coarse blankets, rumpled longish hair. How strange he looked asleep, the green eyes closed. She longed to touch him. She reached out a tremulous hand. "What shall I do now I am here?" she thought. "I should just leave, now that I know he is all right..."

She touched his warm hand. He stirred. She moaned low in her throat, feeling all the mad emotions this boy aroused in her, churning up a storm inside her brain. "I should leave!" she thought.

He opened his eyes.

It seemed that she was drowning in the infinity that lived in those green eyes, shining even in the dimness with their own inner light. She became aware all at once- aware of the darkness surrounding them, night's gentle cloak, the sharp quick sound of their breathing, the rustling movements of the animals, the touch of her hand on his. Her senses sang.

"Jacqueline." He said her name in wonder, as if he thought he was dreaming. He moved his hand, then she felt his strong fingers enclose her own. *Why have I been hiding from myself?* she thought. *Why have I tried to deny it? I love him. I want him.*

She thought this as she looked at him, and it seemed that he could read her heart.

"Why have you come here, Jacqueline?" he said softly.

"Did you know there is pox in the castle?"

"I know." His hand squeezed hers, unsure, gentle, as though their hands were beings apart, groping their way into each other. "I inquired about you. I knew you were all right."

"Oh…" she let out the word in a soft breath. It had not occurred to her that he too might be worried. But how much that meant! He too cared. He cared.

"I was worried about you," she said. "I had to know…"

Now the current altered between them. It was as though they had declared their love for each other and now again something was changed. The thin precarious bond that had formed between them was becoming stronger, pulling tighter, pulling them toward the inevitable. Jacqueline waited, struck with a wild excitement that was not unlike fear.

Guillaume rose from his straw bed, still gripping her hand. He stood before her. She did not move. He groped and found her other hand and held it tightly. Slowly, very slowly, he leaned toward her. She felt his warm breath on her face, his lips touching her forehead, then her mouth. She could hear the violent pounding of his heart mingled with her own. Waves of emotion swept her, making her legs go weak beneath her. He kissed her again, more insistently, forcing her lips open with his tongue. She thought for a moment, No! Then she gave herself to his kiss with a passion as violent, as intense, as anything she had ever known.

After the kiss he drew away. He lay back on his bed and pulled her down beside him. She did not resist.

But it did not happen that night. They lay, fully dressed, in each other's arms, wrapped in the old blanket that smelled of horse and sweat. They lay entwined together in a cocoon woven of their new and tremulous love. In the morning, just before dawn, Jacqueline left him sleeping and crept back to the castle to her chamber. Her love wafted about her like an aura.

Chapter 12

In the bright light of day the aura dimmed and faded. Jacqueline had slept a little upon returning to her room and when she woke, memory flooded her, memory of his kiss, of his warm, hard body next to hers. Her first impulse was that she had dreamed it. Her second was to be horrified. Though she remained a virgin, surely she was defiled. She could never now become a nun. She must submit to her father's wish, and marry.

Then her brain seemed to come awake and with simple clarity she saw that her love for Guillaume was nothing evil. Perhaps it was a sin. Perhaps such a love should not exist. Perhaps the church would not welcome her as a bride of Christ, after she had loved a man. But was it so terrible? They had lain in each other's arms, but as brother and sister, not lovers. Was their love not pure and clean?

She wrestled with the questions. But soon enough the waking castle brought her back to the present reality. A servant-maid, bringing bread for breakfast, whispered through the door, "The lord, your father, has fallen ill." Despite her falling out with her father, the words struck fear into Jacqueline's heart.

If I had known then what my father would later do- would I have wished so fiercely that he would live? the old nun bowed her head in shame. She feared she knew the answer.

When the news of her father's illness was given, Jacqueline and her sisters bowed their heads in a brief, supplicating prayer. Then Joan had asked hastily, "And our brothers?"

"They are well, but they will not leave his bedside."

"We too must go to him," Marie said,

Jacqueline turned to them slowly. "No. You must stay with Ralf and Cecile. Someone must be well to care for them. I will go to our father. Let me. Please." Her eyes pleaded with them. They well knew why she asked it.

"Send him our love and prayers, Jacqueline," Joan said, and turned away.

So she had gone, down the winding passageways to her father's chambers. The heavy door opened to reveal a pale and waxy figure stretched out on the bed. He moaned once every while. Antoine and Louis sat nearby, one on each side of the bed, one at the foot. They looked up together as their sister entered.

"How long?" She asked in a whisper.

Louis answered. "Only this morning. He appeared to be well last night."

"My brothers. We must pray for him." Her voice broke on the last word. Antoine, the silent one, took her hand. His comfort flowed into her, and she composed herself.

They prayed a long while, knowing it was the most important thing they could do. They applied what remedies they knew as well. One of the children always kept vigil by the father's bedside. They tried to feed him a little. On the third day of his illness he swallowed some broth. Jacqueline, alone with him in the room, was feeding him. The room was dim with evening and candlelight flickered on her father's face. For the first time since the illness had fallen, he appeared to become fully conscious. He opened his eyes and looked at his daughter. Then he smiled and mumbled, "Lina." Her heart overflowed. He had called her by the pet name of her childhood. A moment later he fell into unconsciousness again, but it was the turning point of his illness. From then on, he improved.

Toward the end of Lord Bonel's sickness, as he lay in bed recovering, a fresh blow struck. Young Cecile fell ill. No one knew how she had been exposed, for the children's chambers had been quarantined from the first outbreak of the pox. Perhaps a servant had inadvertently carried the dread disease along with the daily meal.

Jacqueline, whose heart had lightened with the recovery of her father, felt a weight of lead upon it again. Her young sister was a sweet and lively child, very intelligent and quick. She looked more like their mother than any of the other children. *Is it a punishment for my sin?* Jacqueline thought guiltily. *Surely God could not be so cruel!* But she remembered Robert and wondered.

They all threw themselves tirelessly into the care of the sick child. They put Ralf in a separate room, and prayed that he too would not fall ill. With all their skill and hope, they nursed Cecile. But the pink cheeks faded into ghostly pallor, and the red blossoms of the pox bloomed on her soft skin. She could neither eat nor drink, and every breath was harsh and labored. It soon became evident that she could not live, though the family still hoped for a miracle.

At this time the pressure and pain of waiting for the child to die overwhelmed Jacqueline with a need for someone to comfort her. She did not think of God in her need. She thought of Guillaume. She longed to see him- yes, to have him hold her, kiss her, make her forget her worry, the searing pain....

Marie relieved Jacqueline of the vigil by Cecile's bedside late the next afternoon. Instead of resting, Jacqueline slipped outside. In the turmoil of Cecile's illness it was not hard to do.

Guillaume was sitting on a mound of hay in the stables eating his supper. It seemed so homey, so natural a scene, that Jacqueline almost laughed with relief. Perhaps the pox was a dream, only a nightmarish dream, and all was well within the eternal stone walls of the castle…

He gazed at her in amazement, then grinned, holding out a piece of bread as an offering. She went to him and took it, smiling too. They ate silently, then he said, "What brings you here?"

This question brought her back to reality. "Guillaume," she said. How few times she had ever called his name aloud! Yet how often she had spoken it in her heart.

"My young sister Cecile has the pox."

He stayed silent for a moment, then his hand closed over hers. His current flowed into her, and she felt a flush of warmth.

"I needed your comfort," she said softly, not looking into his deep-seeing eyes.

There was a movement at the door. Jacqueline jumped, and Guillaume pulled his hand sharply away from hers. They both looked into the harsh face of her brother, Antoine.

"Sister!" His voice was angry, accusing. "We have been searching for you." Then in a gentler tone, "She is dead."

Jacqueline took in the meaning of his words silently. Bitterness numbed her, and she felt strangely calm.

"Let us go into the castle, then," she said. They left the stables without looking back.

Chapter 13

Jacqueline waited for the ax to fall. Antoine's bitter accusing eyes on her were very painful, for she loved her kind, silent brother. He knew of her and Guillaume, it was clear. Perhaps he had not named the bond between them—but he had seen them sitting close together, maybe had even seen them touching hands. Her face burned when she thought of it. He must have told their father; or perhaps he was waiting for the grief over Cecile to pass. She had little doubt that the blow would come. Her punishment was almost upon her.

It hurt all the more that she felt guilt as well as grief for her young sister. *I should have been there,* she thought, chastising herself that she had not been. *Why am I never there when someone beloved to me dies?*

Ah, but once I was there, the old nun thought. *I should not have been there. It almost destroyed me, for it killed all the love in me. I hated for a long and bitter time.*

She tried to brush the thoughts aside. There was far too much time for thinking now that she was old and her tasks were over. She longed for the service at Nones to soothe her with ancient familiar ritual. In the cool stone chapel, with the sea of nuns around her, she could lose her own vivid identity and blend her being into that of one more eternal, ever loving. She sighed gladly as the distant bells rang to announce Nones. The sound of the footsteps of the young novice who aided her could be heard on the narrow stairs.

The pox passed by after it had cast its final shadow, leaving the castle sparse and empty, under a pall. It was long in lifting, and the remaining occupants never forgot. The ghosts of the dead children seemed to play in the echoing halls.

One day a few weeks later, as the first pale buds of spring opened their faces to the sun, Antoine went to Jacqueline. She saw him walking resolutely toward her, and her heart jumped in fear. She stopped her task, and folded her hands in her lap. At least she must give the appearance of calm.

"May I speak with you, sister?" he said as he drew near. There was no anger in his voice. She nodded, and he sat down beside her.

"I am afraid I blamed you for Cecile," he started haltingly.

"Why?" She asked, startled. She had not expected this.

"You should have been with her."

"But I was! I sat with her all day; Marie had just come."

"Please," Antoine held up his hand. "Do not defend yourself. There is no need. I was wrong to blame you. I only felt- bitter." He was silent for a long moment. "You knew how much I loved her. And she was so... so like our mother."

It was true. The tall, quiet Antoine and the bright chattering child had been very close. And Cecile had been much like Lady Bonel in her younger days. Antoine had been but a child, yet he remembered. He had mourned their mother very deeply.

"Yes, I know," Jacqueline said gently.

"But that is not really what I wanted to say," he said. Jacqueline's heart chilled again. She waited.

"Why were you in the stables that day?" Antoine's voice was low, questioning rather than accusing. He did not meet her eyes.

"To see to my horse." The answer sounded curt and false even to her own ears. Her brother met her eyes then. She looked away.

"What gives you the right to ask me this? I need not tell you." She could feel the tense anger in her voice. After all, Antoine was young, younger than she. Close in age to Guillaume, though her brother somehow seemed older.

"Was it to see him?" His voice was strangely gentle.

"Well... we have struck up a friendship of sorts," she said cautiously. Perhaps a partial truth would do.

"I see. A friendship."

"Antoine, what right do you have to question me? I am your eldest sister, after all. I cared for this household and for you for a long, long time after our mother..." her voice trailed off, then she went on, "I have done nothing wrong."

"Perhaps I have no right, Jacqueline," he said earnestly. "Except I am your brother and must guard your honor."

She felt as though he had struck her a blow. Was her honor besmirched then, because she loved a stable boy? Though the answer angered her, she knew the truth. People would think it so.

"Antoine, my honor is not defiled merely because I deigned to speak to a stable boy." The only way to put him off was to play lightly with her real feelings, but she felt as though she was betraying that deep, true bond.

"Yes, that is true," Antoine looked thoughtful. "So you swear there is nothing between you, sister?"

"Nothing," she answered, almost choking on the word. He brother did not see her distress.

He sighed. "I am glad." He kissed her cheek. "I must be off, I will see you at supper."

She sat for a long time after he left, a myriad of emotions churning inside her. "This should not be!" she thought angrily. "I should not have to lie! I love him. That is not wrong."

And she remembered her wish to be a nun. And she wept inside herself, though without tears.

Chapter 14

The old nun sighed, then opened her eyes to the morning. Light flooded the cramped, dull room, making it almost beautiful. She had grown fond of it. It had sheltered her these many years. Somehow, places had always seemed to possess souls and personalities. This room, for instance. It was dull, and quite old, like her. Like her, it had its memories.

The stables where Guillaume worked, ate, slept, had a warm animal smell that had made her, a high-born lady who had always lived in comfort, feel so at home. Even after, whenever she smelled horses or sweet hay, the burning pain came to her belly, the terrible hurt of wanting to see Guillaume, to touch him…and that could no more ever be.

And the immense castle where she had been born, where she had lived as a child, where she had become a woman—she had loved the castle too. It had seemed like an immense protective being that watched over her family, and saved them from their enemies. It was years, many long, long years, since she had been within those high walls. Yet she remembered with a pang the cold nights by the fire, embroidering with her sisters, the gay holidays of her early childhood, with all the family about. Do all old people recall their long-gone childhoods as happy? There was no way to know. The nuns did not speak of such things. There was love between the sisters, but it was a communal feeling, not a bond between individuals. Friendship was frowned upon. Even the relationship with Mother Alfreda had been looked at askance. Jacqueline had learned to live with it, for loving had brought her such pain. She had longed to throw herself into the multitude of nuns, to merge her identity utterly. But she had learned that God could not be served by a non-entity, only by a whole person who was joyous in her work, and who loved the holy life. She was grateful to the other nuns that she had learned it.

Places. The wood, the blessed wood, where she had seen her vision. There all was pure and clear. She thought of it as a holy place. And when the sun's last lingering rays spread over the distant purple hills, and the birds outside her window sang to the evening, that too was holy.

But people? She had so often pondered what lay in the souls of other people. Their thoughts, their inner beings, remained inscrutable. Even Guillaume, whom she had come to know so well, she had not always understood. She had begun, after long years of living, to know herself. Now, in her great age, there were still mysteries about her. It is the task of a lifetime to learn to understand oneself, she had often thought. And she marveled in God's creations. There were times when every breath, every heartbeat, seemed a miracle.

Chapter 15

For the first time in many years there was to be a large May Day celebration in Lord Bonel's household. He himself had decreed it, saying that it was well deserved after the hard winter and the sadness the pox had brought. Besides, there were special friends he desired to entertain.

All who lived in the castle were excited, down to the lowliest servants, who would have some escape from the endless dreary routine. Marie and Joan were the most eager for the holiday because their father had hinted that there would be eligible men, the sons of the nobility. But a little of their gladness was quelled, for they knew the moment to end Jacqueline's dreams had come.

When the blow came, Jacqueline had expected it for so long that it was somewhat subdued. She knew that the man her father had chosen for her would be at the celebration. Many families were traveling long distances to be at Lord Bonel's gathering, even including some distant cousins of the king. Jacqueline must play the role of lady and daughter of a wealthy lord to the hilt, a model daughter, obedient to her father's wishes. A role her heart cried out against-but she would play it. Yet it would be only a role. She would still find a way to follow God's calling.

So she threw herself into the preparations. She supervised the cooks as they made ready the most delectable foods; galantine pie, smoked pike, roast salmon, baked chicken, currant rice, leeks with walnuts, spiced eggs, sorrel soup, cream sauces, parsley bread, mulled wine, and fantasy shapes made out of marzipan. She supervised the cleaning of the great hall, and the decorating with flowers and sweet rushes. She received the minstrels who had come to provide music. And when the guests began to arrive, she played her role as eldest daughter perfectly. She received them, made polite conversation, and provided good meals and comfortable accommodations, since many families were staying at the castle for weeks. She noticed that there were many young unmarried men among these families. She treated all of them courteously, but retained her distance.

Marie had been quickly courted by one of the men, young Lord Delon, whose father held a high post in the French government. Lord Delon was rather affected, having spent time at court and learned such ways, but he was courteous and handsome. Marie felt she was much in love, and went about in a daze of happiness. She was quick to tell all who would listen how he quoted sonnets to her, and how Queen Eleanor herself had never had a more chivalrous lover.

Jacqueline watched Marie with her young man, and Joan and the two older boys with the other young people who had come with their families, and felt both pleased and annoyed. It was right that her brothers and sisters should have such attentions, especially the twins, for they were at a suitable age for marriage. They were both quite pretty, with even features, large hazel eyes, well-molded lips, and fair hair. They were both intelligent, lively, and they deserved happy lives. They both wanted marriage and children. And yet Jacqueline was annoyed. This was not the life she herself wanted. She would have preferred there to be no party. She would have preferred to enjoy the quiet peace of early May alone. She wanted to walk through the flowering fields on a warm day after her work was done and just think. Instead, she must dress in fine clothes and the elaborate headdress that was in fashion, and make meaningless talk with her father's friends.

And beneath the simple annoyance was the fear. Among these people was the sealer of her doom.

There was one other who was not pleased with the coming May Day celebrations. That was Guillaume. He was working very hard to care for all the extra horses put in his charge, though he did have the help of some of the boys who worked in the castle. And he too knew that Jacqueline's husband-to-be was among the visitors. He bitterly hated every young man who rode through the gates, young men on fine horses, dressed in fashionable clothes, one of them come to take Jacqueline away.

She in the castle and he in the stables, and their minds bound together as one. After only two days of greeting guests and seeing to their comforts, Jacqueline's tongue burned with the trite words she had to speak, and her mind dwelled on Guillaume's image. She must see him. The thought seemed more and more immediate. *For,* she thought in sorrow and bitterness, *it may be the last time. I may soon be married.*

Complaining of illness, she asked Marie to take over the guests for the day. Marie was a pleasing hostess, and she loved the color and excitement of having company to liven up their somewhat dreary lives. Jacqueline rested that day and then, as night fell and the guests were at supper, she put on an old dress and cloak, drew the hood over her face, and slipped out of some little-used doors to the stables.

Night had just fallen and the air had a sharp chillness. She could smell the sweet scent of the newborn spring flowers wafting to her on a light breeze. Overhead the stars were brilliant, seeming close enough to touch. She breathed in deeply the sweetness of the spring night. Voices came to her from inside the great hall, where family and friends were supping. She tried to block out the noise, but the sweetness of the night was spoiled. She went into the stables.

He was not there. She waited inside the doorway, then called softly. Her horse recognized her voice and neighed to her. Some of the other horses called out in answer. But Guillaume did not answer.

This had never happened before and she was not sure what to do. The disappointment struck her so deeply she wanted to cry out with the pain of it. She hugged herself tightly, as if in comfort, and settled down to wait.

As time passed, she grew restless. People may be drifting up to bed, she feared, though usually the revels went on for hours. What if Marie or Joan decided to check on her and found her gone from her pallet? She calmed herself by considering that they would stay up as late as possible in the company of their young men, and her father would encourage the dalliance.

And my love, she thought bitterly. *I must wait for him in stables. I must steal moments.*

Guilt smote her briefly. She had been brought up to do as her parents bid. Perhaps it was a sin to dally with a stable boy. Why did she simply not put him from her mind, and try with all her being to do as her father asked?

But Jacqueline was willful, and she obeyed the dictates of God and her own heart. Perhaps this was wrong, but deep inside she did not feel it to be so. She tossed her brief guilt into the breeze and let it blow where it would.

Chapter 16

Jacqueline waited until she could no longer. She got up to return to the castle, but the disappointment was too keen. *I must see him tonight,* she thought. *What if there is no other chance? I must look for him.*

Then she remembered the secret way into the castle. Might he be there? The idea stirred her to excitement. Yes, perhaps....she fairly ran out of the stables into the night. Outside, she stopped short, hearing voices. She drew back into the shadows and listened intently. Was it him?

But no. Two young boys came into view, those who were helping Guillaume with the horses. For a brief second she wanted to show herself, call out to them, "Where is he?" but she stopped herself. They entered the stables and she ran toward the castle kitchens.

It did not take her long to find the entrance that Guillaume used, near to the kitchens. She smoothed her rumpled hair, rearranged her hood, and slipped through.

The corridor was dim, but she heard voices, low and laughing. Could Guillaume be making conversation with the kitchen servants? He must have friends among them, though it was a thought that had not occurred to her before. She went toward the voices she heard and listened. Yes, one voice was Guillaume's. But who was the other? Someone she could trust not to speak?

The folly of the situation occurred to her. She could so easily be caught. But the thought disturbed her no more than a butterfly that flits by and is gone. When Guillaume was near all other reality faded away. His reality was sharp as a sword. There was only him. Only him.

She peered around the corner into the light. A candle flickered from a groove in the wall. Guillaume was crouched on the ground, laughing. Beside him, close beside him, was a young servant girl who helped in the kitchen. Her hair hung loose and her dress was rumpled.

It took Jacqueline a moment to breathe. Not this, never this. In a million years, a million dreams, she had not thought of this. Only he existed for her- for his sake, even her desire to serve God had lessened. For him, a mere peasant boy. What was she to him? Someone to play with, to laugh with and forget, she, the daughter of the house? She stepped into the light. He saw her. He stared in shock, then leaped up, leaving the servant girl to her startled thoughts. But Jacqueline had already fled.

She heard his mad, pounding steps behind her, and she ran, without knowing her destination. She ran outside, past the stables, toward the outer castle wall. She pushed through the inner gate and kept running. All her mind told her to flee, to leave the killing pain behind. All her sinews, every muscle, worked toward one goal- to get away.

And yet his footsteps followed her, and she heard his voice call her name frantically over and over.

Then she stumbled and fell. She lay stunned for a moment, then tried to rise and run again, but he had caught her. He held her arm tightly.

"Jacqueline," he said. He was crying. She was stunned by his tears. She had never seen a man cry.

"Jacqueline, understand, please. I know you must marry. I can never have you. Your future husband is here already. I can never have you. I must try to forget you. But I cannot. I only think of you. I am with someone else, and I think of you. But I must forget you, because you are a lady, and you will marry a great lord…."

He was breathing hard and she looked at him, making out his brilliant eyes in the dim moonlight. Her heart pounded so violently, she gave in to her weakness, and sank to the ground.

"Guillaume, who was she?" She pushed the words out in a whisper.

"No one. A servant girl. I thought you would be with- him. I never thought you could get away tonight. I was with her, trying to forget about you! I thought I would never see you again!"

Then his voice lost its pleading. He looked at her and his eyes bored into her. "You know I speak the truth."

"Yes."

They sat in the damp grass until their harsh breathing slowed. Jacqueline sat, knowing something had changed. He was not as innocent as she had thought. And another new thing; she was sure now. He did love her. He loved her. And something would happen. She could feel it now, between them…..

She thought of this as she sat, waiting. *I was to be a nun, a virgin dedicated to God. I could be a great lady, wealthy, with a rich and handsome husband. Yet, I give it up for him. My family would be shocked if they knew. The virtuous Jacqueline! These thoughts would never have disturbed my mother's tranquil mind. She would be shocked at what I am doing…*

Jacqueline's thoughts came in tumultuous spurts, mingling and flowing in a rushing stream. All the while her blood was pulsing through her veins, making her so warm…Strange feelings made waves running through her belly and legs. She did not push the feelings away, as before. She let them wash over her, dulling her conscious mind until she was a being rocked with sensation, waiting.

He unhooked her cloak and spread it on the ground. He pushed her hair back from her face, gently, with both hands. He slipped off his tunic, then his shirt. He was thin. Hard muscles rippled beneath his palely gleaming skin. She watched him, not stirring, fearful, yet accepting the inevitable. Nothing else seemed to matter, not even her fear.

He knelt beside her and loosened her dress. He knew exactly how to do it. She felt it slip off her shoulders. She gasped and held it to her. His eyes met hers for a moment, his speaking eyes. They spoke to her in a strange language, one she had never heard before, but that she understood. She resisted no longer.

Then, she covered herself with the cloak and watched him. She had never seen the male body before. He looked beautiful to her. He lay next to her and pushed the cloak aside. They did not feel the chill air. Where he touched her, her flesh burned. She blanked her mind, giving herself up to the pleasure and the pain, the pleasure and the pain that intermingled and became one.

After, a calm peace descended upon her. Her being was no longer rocked in storm, but rested in tranquil waters. The moon shone down upon the two as they lay. The moon is like a blessing, she thought.

"I love you," he said to her. She gave her vows in turn. She felt utter peace. She would lay forever next to him; she would die here. She wanted nothing else at all from life.

It was Guillaume who stirred first. "You must be getting back," he said. She was hardly aware of dressing, hardly conscious of entering the castle walls. She was different, she was changed. She was not only herself now- she was Guillaume too. He was part of her, and she of him.

Guillaume came as near to the castle as he dared, and kissed her goodnight. "I will see you, my love," he vowed. "They will not stop us. I will see you."

Jacqueline crept up to the chamber she shared with her sisters. Consciousness was beginning to dawn. What could she say if her sisters were there? What hour was it? She had no awareness of how long she had been gone.

But though the time with Guillaume had seemed to last an eternity, only a few hours had passed. People still filled the banquet hall, and the bedchamber was empty.

Jacqueline lay down, and she slept, but her dreams were troubled, and she saw blazing fires that ravaged flowered fields, and fleeing people that filled her brain with their terrible cries.

Chapter 17

In the morning what she had done seemed terrible to her. She had lost what she could never, never get back and she had given up her great dream forever. God would not have her now. Neither could any husband have her. She was utterly defiled.

And yet, the sweetness that rose in her loins when she thought of his slender body, his touch....she prayed to God as she had never prayed before, asking him to let her forget. But God did not answer, and the lust remained, burning in her like a sickness.

It was doubly hard because again she had to sit with her father's guests, talk with them, eat with them, pretend she was interested in their concerns and their idle chatter. And all the time her body ached with remembering, and her mind was tortured with her sin.

But it was almost impossible to bear when, smiling broadly, her father came to her to introduce a young man who had just arrived, a pallid-looking, stiff young man who was the son of a prominent noble on a nearby estate. "May I present my daughter, Lady Jacqueline," Lord Bonel's voice was full of pride.

Jacqueline made her bows, and he, his. "So this," she thought, "is the man my father has chosen for me." Her heart cried out for Guillaume.

"You keep a fine table, Lady," the young man was saying. "The banquet will surely be quite grand."

Jacqueline consciously forced an answer from her reluctant throat. "Thank you, my lord. Yes, I am looking forward to the banquet." No, she could not continue. "Pray excuse me, my lord, I must see to supper."

He inclined his head graciously, and she moved slowly away. When she saw that his eyes were no longer on her, she made her escape, fleeing to the sanctuary of her bedchamber. She sat on her pallet and closed her eyes, pressing her hand to her heart. She felt ill. For the first time the thought occurred to her; could she be with child? The thought struck her dumb. If so, then it was over. Everything was over. Her life was over.

And Guillaume? His life would be over too. If she were with child, the father of the child would not go unpunished. How long before they would all know? But pray God it was not so. Perhaps her illness only stemmed from the knowledge that time was catching up to her. How could she marry now? Yet, here was her father, smiling broadly, with a young man in tow, a very good match, son of a nobleman. How would she be able to refuse him? How could she defy her father?

She sent word that she felt ill, and would not attend supper that night.

The old nun sat by her window, gazing out at the chill November evening. The day was All Soul's Day. She had prayed for those whom she had loved. She did not even know whether her brothers and sisters were still alive after so many years. So she prayed for them all. Especially for Guillaume.

November had a haunted aura about it, a time when life wrapped itself in a cocoon for winter. She loved the look of skeletal trees against the gray sky, loved the bare brown look of the land. Spirits seemed to dance under the naked trees on this All Soul's Day, calling for the living to remember. The spirits of all those she had loved....Guillaume....

The banquet day had come. The tables were laden with magnificent food, the Maypole was up, waiting for the young unmarried men and women to tie ribbons around it. People were dressed in their gay best, and the castle was swarming with color and noise and excitement. Jacqueline moved through it all in a numb state. If she thought too much about what had happened with Guillaume she would go mad. So she buried all thought in the attic of her mind. She did her duty as hostess, with the help of her sisters. She said the proper words. The color and excitement of the day was like a dream so vivid it became a nightmare.

Jacqueline was seated at the banquet next to Lord Courcy, according to her father's wishes. As the wine flowed, his tight polite talk became bolder. At first Jacqueline has given short trite answers, but his new words shook her out of her painful reverie.

"Lady," he was whispering. "Dare I call you Jacqueline? A name that trips off the tongue. You are very lovely. What say we slip away after, into the garden? Tonight...tonight will be a night for love..."

Lord Courcy's words sickened her. They were like a desecration. She was no innocent anymore- oh, no, she had known physical love. And though she knew it was a sin, at least it had been with someone she loved with a passion that frightened her. For this pallid man to suggest she share such an intimate thing with him; it was too much. She felt a shock run through her at his words.

"I will not stomach such talk!" she cried, almost too loudly. She put down her cup of wine with a slam, so that some spilled onto the table.

Lord Courcy grew embarrassed. "I am sorry, my Lady," he sputtered. "I meant no harm. Only that I forget myself in your presence." Jacqueline paid no heed. He was a smooth talker; so different from Guillaume! His words had meaning because he loved her. This one only wanted something from her. Thinking of Guillaume, of what had happened between them, a flush went over her. She shuddered lightly, feeling a sudden confusion. She loved Guillaume, but she was promised to this young man. She must not forget that, and she must not make an enemy of him.

Jacqueline turned to the flustered young lord, trying to make amends. "I am sorry. Perhaps we may dance together later."

"Yes, yes, my Lady. I have been too bold. Later we will dance."

After the feast, the tables were cleared and room was made ready for dancing. The lute players arranged themselves and began to play, and all over the great room the young men and women paired off for the dance. Jacqueline had hidden herself in a corner, but she knew could not remain hidden. Lord Courcy would find her, and she would have to submit to the ordeal of dancing with him.

In the meantime she listened to the songs. After the first rousing number, a lone minstrel came forth to sing. A hush fell over the assembled company at his first tones. His voice was high and sweet with youth, and he sang with the anguish of a love forever lost.

"Fair was my love, with golden hair

And skin as soft as an angel's wing…"

Something caught in Jacqueline's throat as she heard the words, listened to the tune, so mournful and haunting. It was like a premonition. Her love for Guillaume, so sweet, so intense, could never be fulfilled. But yet how she loved him! The song of love brought back the memory of that night of love so intensely that she could feel his warm hands on her bare skin, hear the words he had spoken to her, soft and low, words of love and longing. The tears burned her eyes, threatening to spill. She wanted him, she longed for him! She was aware of nothing but this burning longing.

"And I will not see her again, my love. No, I will ne'er see her again."

She sat numb after the song had ended. Guillaume. She must see him. She must be with him again, touch him…

"Lady," a voice said softly. She was startled out of her dream. She looked into the face of Lord Courcy. The sight sickened her. And yet, she must be polite, be kind, hide the emotions she had been feeling.

"Yes, my lord. I had been listening to the song." Her voice sounded strained even to her ears.

"A lovely song. But it is no night for sadness. Come. You promised me a dance."

Jacqueline rose, somewhat unsteadily. He clasped her hand to assist her. She almost froze at his touch, wanting nothing more than to back away and run, as far as she could go. She forced herself to move forward with him, hoping he would not notice her revulsion.

Apparently, warmed by the wine and the music, he did not. He moved into the dance, bringing her with him. She could do nothing but follow his lead. She began to feel a kind of detachment from what she was doing. Jacqueline was there on the dance floor with Lord Courcy, making the movements of the dance. But that Jacqueline was only a shadow. The real Jacqueline was in the stables with Guillaume, her love. Her own love. She would never forsake him for this one who danced and drank and mouthed words he did not mean. Never. She would find a way.

That night the old nun had a dream. At first there was light and beauty. There was a banquet table laid out with myriads of wonderful food, and laughing people all around. Then the scene altered. The people were gathered together to watch a burning. Jacqueline was among them. She strained her eyes to see who was to meet that terrible fate. She looked at the scaffold. The flames had begun to rise and she heard terrible screams, unearthly screams, of someone in the depths of torment. In the midst of the fire was Guillaume's face, but it was melting away…

She awoke covered in a chill sweat. After so many years, he still haunted her. She slept no longer that night, as the November wind sang eerily at her window.

Chapter 18

Jacqueline opened her eyes. Outside the narrow window the moon shone with frosty brilliance. The full moon. She started in panic. She was to meet Guillaume that night, for they had bargained to meet when next the moon was full. Though she had pondered on the wisdom of it, after that Mayday evening, when her passion had calmed a little, she knew she could not stay away. A mere chance glimpse of him readying some horses for the guests had been enough to make her blood boil again, to make her yearn for his touch. And so, in hasty whispers, they had contrived to meet again when the moon was full. And the night had arrived.

It is only a matter of time until I am caught, Jacqueline thought in pain. *How then will I see him? My father will marry me off in a hurry to a man I despise.* She got up, moving carefully, slowly, so her sisters, sleeping nearby, would not be aroused. She crept from her pallet and flung on her cloak. She moved to the window.

It was May but the nights were chill, and the rush of cool air met her. With the full moon shining she could see the curve of the distant hills and the dark shape of the trees where the woods began. She gasped at the sheer beauty of the scene, and raised her eyes to the moon itself. *What is it,* she thought suddenly, *what is this great light in the sky that changes shape and sometimes cannot be seen at all? Is it large or small, and what are those dark forms all over its surface?*

Jacqueline was startled by her own thoughts. She had not questioned the physical world before, only accepted it. But now, as she gazed intently at the moon, an unbidden thought arose; surely there was a God, for such beauty to exist.

Thinking this, she bowed her head in shame. *I should not have forgotten my calling. How easily I forgot!*

She looked up at the blazing moon almost fiercely. *I shall forget no longer!* She vowed silently. She clutched her hands together in prayer. She would not go to meet Guillaume that night.

But, as Jacqueline gazed out at the beauty of the night, unable to leave the window, one of her sleeping sisters stirred and opened her eyes. Joan was startled by the figure at the window, and almost cried out before the light of the moon showed her the profile of her sister Jacqueline. She lay still, pondering. She knew that her sister sometimes slipped from her bed in the dark night of night, although Joan had told no one, not even her twin. And she had begun to suspect the truth of the entire matter. Yet she had said nothing. Now it was time to speak.

Joan too arose quietly, so as not to rouse the more innocent Marie. She went up to Jacqueline and called her name softly.

Startled out of reverie, Jacqueline gasped and turned. Seeing Joan she felt guilty, afraid that Joan knew where she had been going before the shining moon changed her mind. "I could not sleep," she whispered, trying to calm her pounding heart.

"Jacqueline," Joan began, "Sister...is that truly why you are up tonight?"

Jacqueline met her eyes with a feeling of horror so deep it was almost peaceful. Calmness descended upon her.

"Why do you ask, Joan?"

Joan seized the moment. "I have seen you. I have seen you leave your bed at night. At first I thought you were sleeping badly, but then I wondered. You spurn Lord Courcy's advances and ... and I have heard no more talk of your becoming a nun." She took Jacqueline's cold, limp hands in hers.

"Oh, tell me, Jacqueline, what has happened to you?"

"I must not tell, I must not falter," Jacqueline thought, though all her being yearned to pour out her pain and guilt to her sister.

"Is it..." Joan halted, groping for words. "Do you have...?"

"A lover?" the words were said and Jacqueline had said them. She willed herself to be strong.

"It is Guillaume, is it not?" Joan said very softly.

"How did you know?" He voice was dull.

"I saw you go to the stables one night. I saw the look in your eyes last week, when we went riding and he readied your horse."

"Joan, I have fallen. It has happened. There, now you know all." Still Jacqueline's voice was dull and cold. Her sin deserved worse punishment than this kind, curious sister's gentle questions. She almost wanted to shock Joan into hatred and disgust.

Joan peered at her closely. The moonlight revealed no emotion on the cold marble face. *She is beautiful in the moonlight,* Joan thought irrelevantly.

"You have... you are no longer a maid?"

"No! I am defiled." Jacqueline spoke roughly.

"Hush! Do not wake Marie. She would not understand."

"She? And you do understand?" Her voice was cynical. Joan had never heard her sister speak so.

"Jacqueline, hush. It was wrong. I do not deny that. But...I do understand." Her voice grew soft. "I too am in love. I know how you feel."

For the first time Jacqueline turned to survey her sister. "Who?" she said, and her voice had grown gentler.

"Master Tormaine," Joan said. "You have met him. He is handsome and so kind. He composes pretty poetry and is so gallant. He is not wealthy, like the man Father has chosen for you…" She realized her mistake as Jacqueline paled, but went on, "But he is a respected merchant, and owns a goodly household. He will ask for my hand soon. He has told me so. You see, I do understand."

"But Joan, it is different. The one I love is not a respected merchant, he is a mere stable boy. How can I wed? I do not want to wed! My husband would want a maid, untouched. And I…." Her face burned and she turned back toward the window, but continued speaking, as though to herself. "I so wanted to be a nun. And I can be nothing now. There is no place left for me. I may as well go to Guillaume. I may as well take what pleasure I can."

"Jacqueline, no, please! Set your mind on marriage, it will not be so bad."

"I thought I could, but I cannot. Could you, loving your Master Tormaine, wed another?"

Joan was silent for a moment. Then she whispered, "No." They did not speak for awhile. Then Jacqueline turned to Joan again.

"You will not tell Father?"

"Never, I swear."

Jacqueline kissed her sister's cheek in a rush of painful affection. She did not deserve such goodness, but she feared her father terribly.

"Goodnight."

"Goodnight, Jacqueline."

As they closed their eyes to sleep a gray cloud drifted over the face of the brilliant moon.

Chapter 19

The days passed. Mayday over, the guests slowly began to disperse back to their own households. Before they left, the betrothal of Lady Joan Bonel to Master Edmund Tormaine was announced. Joan looked more beautiful than ever in her happiness, Marie shone with joy for her twin, and their brothers made bawdy jokes. Lord Bonel looked happier than he had in years. The wedding was to take place in early October. Everyone was pleased, it seemed. But over the pleasure for her sister was a shadow, for Jacqueline knew that her marriage could not be much longer in coming.

Lord Courcy was among the last of the guests to leave. "I will soon return," he whispered to Jacqueline before he left, a large smile on his broad face. "I will return to speak to your father."

Jacqueline's heart pounded in fear, but she held her emotions tightly in check, saying goodbye to him coolly. She walked with him to the courtyard. There stood Guillaume, holding the horses of Lord Courcy and his party.

Again her heart leaped painfully, and she pressed her hand to her chest. She must have looked pale, for Lord Courcy cried, "Are you so distraught then at my leaving, Lady?" He was delighted at the prospect. "Do not fear, I shall return!" Pleased with his theatrics, he clutched her hand and kissed it resoundingly. "Until better things," he murmured and she blushed more in anger than embarrassment. And, laughing, he took the reins of his horse from the stable boy who held them, not seeing the look of burning hatred that that stable boy gave him. Lord Courcy's companions gathered around, mounting their horses, laughing at the scene that they had just witnessed. Waving, shouting, they galloped away.

Guillaume stood alone. Jacqueline faced him. Then she turned and with a stately walk, entered the castle.

That night Jacqueline lay sleepless, but waking dreams disturbed her, sharp thoughts pierced her mind. She thought of Guillaume's face that day, his hatred for the pretty nobleman, his accusing looks at her. She felt angry with him, unexplained anger. And yet, how the sight of him had made her blood boil! Her mind could dwell on nothing else. *It is evil!* she thought. Yet she could not forget. She thought of Lord Courcy, and hated him for his shallowness, his showing off. *I shall never marry!* she thought. But what could she do? Guillaume.....

Jacqueline fell at last into a light and fitful sleep, torturing thoughts still carving their images on her brain. Then, through her dreams, she heard a tapping sound. A scaffold, they were building a scaffold! Who was to burn? I am to burn! Tap, tap...

She opened her eyes. What a fearful dream! She felt sweat upon her forehead. Then a soft sound fell upon her ears. The window. Fearful, yet knowing, she crept softly to it. She pushed open the shutters.

"I had to come." His voice, low and warm, reached her ears. He was grasping the window ledge tightly.

"How did you..?" He cut off her question.

"I scaled the wall. It was not difficult. There are cracks- it is not high. I had to risk it, to see you."

"Guillaume." It was a moan, a cry of desire, of hopelessness.

"Oh, my love, tell me- you no longer want me, do you? He has won your heart, that ...that bastard with the pretty clothes and the filthy mouth!"

Jacqueline was surprised to hear the harshness in his voice. "No..." she began.

"Yet you did not speak to me in the courtyard today," he accused.

"Guillaume! There are too many eyes watching us!" Her harsh tone matched his. Then all harshness, all anger, melted away. She reached out her hand to him. He took it, kissed the palm hungrily, then slowly, with passion. He looked at her again.

"On the night of the full moon you were to come. What happened?"

She told a half-truth. She could not tell him that Joan knew. "My sister was awake. I could not slip away."

"I missed you." His eyes narrowed with love. "Do not stay away from me, Jacqueline, my love. I want you again."

Her legs seemed to turn to water at his words. "Oh, Guillaume, I want you too," she whispered, almost to herself.

"Please come," he said again, pleading.

"You know I will come." She looked into his green eyes. They seemed to shine with their own inner light.

"I love you," she whispered, and leaned to kiss him.

"Tomorrow then?"

"If I can- yes."

"Goodnight my love. Tomorrow!" His smile was like a sunbeam. He climbed nimbly down the castle wall and walked toward the stables. She watched until his figure faded into blackness. Then, hugging his spirit to her, Jacqueline went to her bed and slept soundly.

Chapter 20

How many different people I have been in one lifetime, the old nun thought, brooding. *Before I met Guillaume I was a creature of spirit, I had tossed off the world, I was one with God. Then, after Guillaume, I was a creature of the body, of lust, of passion. The light of my soul dimmed. And now my body is old, withered, a mere shell. It is my spirit that thrives within me. I yearn to be free of this old shell that long ago caused me so much pain...*

The next night Jacqueline lay in her bed, waiting. Still, her sisters tossed and turned. Finally she heard quiet breathing. Almost too hastily she rose to leave.

"Jacqueline," she heard a whisper. She stopped short. Joan sat up. "Don't go."

She turned on her sister. "I thought you understood."

"I do. But it is still a sin."

Jacqueline's head pounded. Yes, a sin, a terrible sin. She thought of Guillaume, and her loins stirred. She went to her sister and grasped her shoulders.

"Joan, remember your promise."

Joan sighed, knowing she was defeated. "I will not tell Father. I have sworn."

Jacqueline tossed on her cloak and left the room, but the burden of her sister's knowledge weighed upon her, slowing her step. Yet, the prospect of being with him was too exciting to deny. She had lost God forever. She had only Guillaume now, this young boy-devil who tempted her with sweet words and intense green eyes. She hurried to him.

He was waiting for her by the stable door. Now that she saw him, she was suddenly shy. He was her lover, and she had come for love. The thought made her shy, but stirred a powerful excitement in her.

"My love," he whispered, but did not touch her as she slowly drew near. He gazed at her for a long moment. She met his gaze. It seemed for an instant that their minds merged and became one, lingering together in the soft May air.

Then he leaned toward her, kissing her slowly, his mouth covering hers. Slowly, in a promise of what was to come.

He knows just what to do, she thought, without knowing she thought at all, for she was a being of rocking, flowing sensation. He took her hand and led her to his straw pallet.

Moments, the old nun thought. *I have gone over those moments over and over in my mind, until they crystalize in memory. They are so sharp, so clear, they seem to have reality outside of my own mind. Somewhere, in some place beyond time, all these things that are past still happen, endlessly, over and over. Where that is, only God knows. It is my punishment that I remember.*

They clung together on a bed of straw amid the sweat that comes of love. He did things she had never dreamed of, yet she could not deny him, for she was full of love and lust and feelings she could not name. Her mind was numbed. She lay in some strange and wild sea that rocked her madly from shore to shore. He loved her fiercely, deeply, so she could not breathe, and still it went on.

Through all, they professed their love. Their love was a physical thing that wrapped around them like a crystal cocoon. Nothing else existed.

Jacqueline opened her eyes, hearing the cock crow. She looked at their bodies on the pallet, entwined in the breaking light of day like one being. She did not want to move, ever. Close beside her his face was still in sleep, his green eyes closed, his breath rising and falling gently.

Why must I leave him? She thought with a terrible and bitter anguish. *Can we not run away? Can we not run away and live as man and wife? We could have a small farm somewhere...*

She kissed his mouth and he stirred. She was mad, it was mad!

"Guillaume," she called his name softly. He opened his eyes and looked at her, with a smile deep and warm and full of love.

"Let us run away."

Guillaume's eyes widened and he pulled himself up. "What do you mean?"

"Why did we not do it before? You must have some little money saved. I can sell my jewels; I have few, but they are worth something. Oh, Guillaume, I cannot give you up!"

"Jacqueline, you would do this? You would give all of this up for me?"

He wanted to do it! She laughed aloud.

"You are everything to me! Everything."

"And what of your dream?"

A small shadow passed over her eyes. Guillaume saw this shadow. *So that too she has given up for me,* he thought. The thought made him feel awed, humbled.

"Jacqueline, I love you beyond life. If you want this, then I will do it gladly. Gladly!" He grasped her hands, then said, "You must return now, it is getting late." A sudden fear showed in his eyes. "What if your sisters have awakened and found you gone? You have been with me a long while."

"Joan knows."

"What?" She heard alarm in his voice.

"Do not worry, she will not tell. She too is in love. She understands."

"You are certain?"

"I can trust her to help us. And perhaps Marie too."

"Then go, my love. There will be much to prepare." He looked at her, almost disbelieving that such a wonderful thing could really happen. "When shall it be?"

"A week. A week from tonight."

"So soon?"

"Yes. Yes!"

He helped her dress, and with a last lingering kiss she hurried to the castle.

Chapter 21

No one was awake when Jacqueline entered her bedchamber. She lay on the bed, mulling over her plans until it was time to rise. She could hardly think of the night just past. The pleasure was too intense, the thought too sweet. Better to think of the future. Soon…!

And it was later that same day that the long suspended ax fell.

Jacqueline was at her chores. She looked up almost by instinct, sensing someone near. A servant maid drew close.

"My lord wishes to speak with you, lady."

Jacqueline's heart gave a painful leap. *Not now, not now!* she thought wildly. *Not when our plans are made, our vows given.*

She followed the maid to the hall where her father sat alone. She scrutinized his face. There was no anger. He did not know. At least that.

"Sit down, daughter," he addressed her in a formal voice. "I think that this news will please you."

He was pleased, she could see. It showed in his mild eyes. There was no murky turbulence in them, none of the usual shadowed pain. "Lord Courcy spoke to me before he left. He has asked for your hand. He made a trip back to his father's estates, but he will soon return. We will announce your betrothal then."

Jacqueline did not meet his eyes; she could not trust herself to speak.

"Jacqueline?"

"Yes, my lord?"

"Look at me."

She met his eyes slowly. He was momentarily surprised at the look of stark pain in them.

"Father." Her voice was dull and even, but there was an undertone of panic that his heart could hear. "Please. Do not force me to do this, I beg you."

The anger rose in him, as did the memory of a woman dying in childbed, and his children looking on. Jacqueline had been old enough to understand.

"You will marry this man, daughter!" His voice grew softer. "It is an excellent match, better than I ever expected. His father is a prominent nobleman whose lands prosper. Francis is the first-born son. There is even talk of him receiving an appointment at court. You will want for nothing. You cannot throw away this opportunity!"

"Father, please." Her voice was dry with pain.

"You will do as I say! Why do you hesitate? It is your foolish ambition, is it not? I thought that you had given that up. If not, you had better. It must be the way I say."

"No, Father, no. It is just....I cannot.... I do not like him."

"There is someone else." She heard the threat in his voice. "Who is it?"

"No, Father. No one." She forced herself to say the words calmly with all the power of her being. He had come dangerously close. She pushed aside her pain, her fear. She must play his game, for she had something much greater to fear- discovery. She willed the words so hard her head ached.

"I am sorry, Father. I – I know I should not disobey you. But the- well, Lord Courcy was somewhat forward and I…"

"Bah! No matter, he will soon be your husband. He did not force himself in any way?"

"Oh, no."

"I did not think so. He is an upstanding man. He was probably just a bit befuddled by all the wine. Now, I want no more talk against this marriage. None, I warn you. Though of course, you are shy."

She had fooled him! She felt only relief for the lie.

"I am sorry, Father." It would do to be humble.

"There, go, Jacqueline. I understand. You have always been a good daughter."

She felt a mixture of guilt and relief as she left him. But she did not know the seeds of suspicion had been planted in his mind. She had betrayed herself in her horror. She had shown herself to be a woman who had everything to lose if she married this prominent young man. Yet, her father reasoned, what has she to lose, if not a lover?

He stored his doubts away. But the seed was planted, and the seed sprouted roots in the man's troubled mind and grew, too quickly.

Chapter 22

Jacqueline's mind was in turmoil all that day but she vowed to remain steadfast. She had already gone so far. She would repudiate all her teachings, she would pretend, she would falsify herself. As long as in the end, Guillaume was her prize. And now, more than ever, it was vital that they leave, perhaps even within a week, before it was too late to leave at all.

It was already too late, the old nun thought, feeling the old dull pain in her soul. *I had lost him already. His doom was sealed. And by my own words I gave him away. My father saw more than I ever suspected.*

Jacqueline had done all she could to make ready for their trip. She packed a few clothes and necessary items, hiding them in her chamber. She thought out some plans in her mind on where they might go at first, how they would live in the immediate future. But the details did not seem too important. The main thing was to get away. She took her few jewels and hid them carefully among her clothes. At least they would have some money to live on for a time.

The secret she carried made Jacqueline go through the motions of everyday life almost feverishly, burning with the inner excitement of her love. Her father could not spoil it. She would not let him. She would do all she could to behave normally, to do her regular chores, and in the meantime, whenever she had a spare moment, she would prepare for the leaving.

Unbeknownst to her, her father was watching. He saw her high color, her nervousness. And he thought to himself, *it is not because of my news that she behaves this way. Why have I not watched her more closely? She has always been the rebel. If only her mother....my beloved Marguerite. Why were you not here to guide her?*

The bitterness washed over him, the bitterness of losing that wife he had held so dear, losing her because of his own lust. She should not have had more children, and even knowing this, he had....And the bitterness was a poison in him, a spreading poison, and the doubt about his daughter grew.

As night drew near, Lord Bonel spoke to his son, Louis, who was closest to him of all his children.

"I have told your sister of Lord Courcy's request for her hand. Yet she acted strangely, refusing, then apologizing."

"Refusing, Father? A man like him?" Louis was incredulous.

"Yes. And I believe there is a reason. Have you noticed anything, my son?"

Louis was an excellent horseman and was learning to be an excellent fighter, but his mind was plodding and unperceptive. He was often away from home and hardly knew his eldest sister.

"No, Father." Then he remembered something Antoine had said to him awhile before. He had taken little notice at the time, but now, with his father's insinuations, the words took on a new meaning.

"Father, I do recall something. Antoine said…well, it may be nothing, but…"

"What did he say?" There was a venom in Lord Bonel's voice that his son did not hear.

"He said, 'She has lately developed a great love for riding.' He mentioned that it was odd that she had been in the stables when Cecile was so ill."

A shadow fell upon them for a moment, remembering that terrible time. Then Lord Bonel said, "Go and get your brother. Have him come to me."

Antoine hung his head as he approached his father. He did not wish to implicate Jacqueline. He has already said too much to Louis in anger, right after the incident. He thought it best forgotten.

But Louis was eager to hear all, and their father was looking at Antoine with those burning eyes he had learned to fear.

"Tell me what you know, Antoine." The voice was low, threatening. It was no use to deny.

"That day, Father, when- when sickness was in the castle, I found Jacqueline in the stables. That is all. I was angry. I thought she should have been with Cecile. But I was wrong! She had been tired, and needed to get away."

"To get away? And where was she going?"

"I do not know, sir. I do not believe she was going anywhere."

"Then, there is only one thing to do. We will watch her." He fixed his sons with a black and piercing gaze. "We will make certain that she goes nowhere."

Antoine trembled within himself to hear his father's tone, but he had long ago learned to obey without question.

"Antoine, you may go for now. Louis, you will stand guard over your sister's door tonight."

Chapter 23

After the meager supper of break and ale, the young novice helped the old nun ascend the stairs to her tower room. "Why do you live away up here, Sister," the young novice asked, her voice innocent and curious. "Would it not be easier to live on the ground floor?"

"So as to be closer to God," the old nun answered, and chuckled. The novice opened her eyes wide, then laughed, a clear, pealing laugh that rang up and down the narrow stairs.

"Shhh," the old nun whispered, "The silence is still in effect."

"Oh! I always forget!" the novice said, and clamped her mouth shut. But there was a smile upon it still, and on the old nun's face a smile also flickered.

How long did it take before I smiled again, after it happened? She thought. *How long before every breath I took stopped being a painful reminder that I was still alive?*

They reached the door of her room. The old nun sank into her chair gratefully, for even the slim burden of her old bones sometimes weighed heavily upon her. And her thoughts, those were the heaviest of all. "Oh, God," she prayed aloud when the novice had left, "Help me to forget. Let me forgive. Hail, Mary, full of grace…" And it seemed to her that she was standing among high mountains. Over the mountains heavy purple clouds hung, but the rays of the sun were breaking through. The rays reached the mountaintops like gentling hands. Her heart overflowed, and she raised her arms in worship. In her sleep, the old nun smiled.

It was the second night before their flight that Jacqueline was struck with a desire to see Guillaume. Her desire came not only of passion, but for a practical motive. They had yet to make their plans. The specifics of time and place were still too nebulous.

As she went about her work that day, waiting for the coming night, all demons left her. Jacqueline forgot about all else but him, and the new life that was to be for them. Her own spirit was merged with his. Her love for him was her reason for living. *Tonight,* she thought, *tonight I will see him!* She was ablaze with the desire to see him, to look into his green eyes.

That night, as she waited to go to Guillaume, Jacqueline fell into a restless sleep. Vague images floated across her mind, people that looked inhuman, with fires in their bellies and bloated faces. She woke after many hours drenched in the sweat of fear. She lay in the dark, breathing heavily, trying to pray, to dispel the demons that head descended upon her. Then she remembered her mission. She gasped and glanced outside. The moon was lowering; it must be late. In haste she arose and took up her cloak. She would go to Guillaume, her lover. He would dispel the evil spirits. He would set her mind at rest. His love was her prayer now.

She slipped outside her door, out of the darkened castle, to the stables. She ran like one pursued. And this time, eyes pursued her on her journey, though she did not know... the disbelieving eyes of her brother, Antoine.

Chapter 24

In the dark Antoine scarcely breathed. The worst was true. He did not know what to think. He loved his sister; she was wise and kind, and had cared for the household and the younger children with a skill beyond her years. But what she had done was unforgivable. Antoine knew that his most base suspicions were true. He had brushed them from his mind as one would a bothersome fly, not really believing that his father was right. But now they returned full force, and he knew that his sister was running to her lover. And to have chosen such a one as her lover! Perhaps Antoine could have forgiven her if she had chosen a high-born man, who dressed fine, and who whispered pretty words in her ear and made her forget her life of toil. But a stable boy, a straggly youth no older than Antoine himself, a lowly, scurvy... The thought of his high-born and beloved sister in the stable boy's arms roused the mild Antoine to a rage that he had never felt before. In those moments he hated his sister for her weakness. He had thought, when his father set him to this task, that he could never betray his sister. Now, with steady footsteps, he went straight to his father's chamber.

Of all the events of her life, this most important one was the least clear in her mind. All that truly remained of it was a sense of horror so deep that it bit into her brain when thought of it came, unbidden. Somehow she had felt it necessary to remember what had happened, exactly, in sequence. But she only recalled the breaking in, the cries, the hatred that was scented gall upon the very air. She never knew exactly how she was found out, but she had reconstructed the betrayal in her mind. At the very moment that she was with Guillaume, at the very time they clung together and made their hasty plans, one of her brothers was pronouncing Guillaume's death sentence.

They had decided to meet after all had gone to bed the very next night, with only their small bundles of clothing and possessions. This would give Jacqueline time to prepare some food for the journey. The moon would not be too bright, which would assist them in getting away without being seen. They would take the south road, which was the least traveled, to the nearest village. In their old clothes they would blend in with the townspeople there. They would rest, then be off again, perhaps in the company of fellow travelers, which would make their abduction less likely. They thought to buy the cloaks of pilgrims, for no one would bother two pilgrims on their way to the shrine at Canterbury.

They had made their hasty plans, then, in the joy of their love they had clung together. He was never more part of me than at that moment, Jacqueline had thought later, when she could think at all. They were laughing through their kisses, he was holding her, they were so glad to be together....

And then her father had burst in.

Memory was merciful. It had spared her remembrance of the details. She recalled the cries; the cries of her brothers and her father, cries bloated with hatred; the nervous neighs of the horses, who sensed the mad emotions of the men. She had glimpsed their faces, twisted, strange. And she had seen the flash of steel without knowing who held it. But memory was not merciful enough. She would carry the last image of Guillaume on the stable floor, his chest split open, lying in a pool of blood, forever. She wore the image next to her heart, next to her cross. She would never forget.

Jacqueline had felt him stiffen in her arms and pull away. Thankfully, she had not seen his face in those last living moments. She had not seen the horror on his face, and the knowledge, and the dreadful fear. She had seen his face next in death, calm, composed, framed by his blood. She knew someone screamed, not knowing it was herself. She felt sharp blows on her head and face, and blackness washed over her, blackness she would have clung to forever if she could.

But it was not to be. Life in her was not ready to give up its hold. When she woke, Jacqueline learned that her father had banished her. She would never see him again. When her eyes had opened, the misty tearful faces of her sisters had floated above her. They were bathing her swollen face.

"You must leave, Jacqueline," Marie said, sobbing the words. "You must go quickly. Father wants you gone by morning."

"He will hurt you- please, Jacqueline, he is mad! Please go, and be safe!" Joan's face was white with pleading.

They had fixed her food and given her their warmest clothes and their few jewels. They had stripped her of her blood-spattered clothes and dressed her in fresh ones. They had brought young Ralf to kiss her goodbye, and walked with her to the castle gates. They had said goodbye just before the dawn.

"We love you, Lina. We love you." With their love, they had sent her away.

They believed he would kill me and he might have, the old nun thought. *What my sisters did not know is that I would have welcomed it. But they would not let it be so. They believed they were sending me to life when they sent me away. And so it was in the end. So it was.* For the convent and the holy way had been life for her. But life had been a thing of crushing pain when she had walked out of the castle gates for the final time, alone.

PART II
THE JOURNEY

Chapter 25

Jacqueline had walked, moving one foot before the other, not knowing what she did. Instinctively she had turned south, in the direction that she and Guillaume had planned to take before.

She could not think. She could not allow herself to think. Her mind was a whiteness, utterly blank. She ate the food her sisters had given her when the time came to eat. She slept when the time came to sleep. Automatically she performed the rituals of survival.

The days and nights merged into each other. Jacqueline was numb and noticed nothing. She had no plans. She merely lived, not really wanting to be alive at all.

The third night after she was banished was dark and stormy. Alone, Jacqueline had trod the dusty path as the twilight dimmed and faded. She gazed at the treetops still outlined blackly against the sky. Scattered clouds blew out from the place where the sun had set. The May night had strange sounds, distant creaks and moans, lights that played as the mists rolled across the fields. Jacqueline grasped her head with her two hands as if to hold something in that she was threatened with losing. She had lost so much already. She could not lose herself too. She wrapped her cloak tightly against her, as though it would contain her fear. A high wind rose, blowing the cloak away from her, flapping it around loosely. The wind sang in her ears, a haunting melancholy tune. The rain started, large, chill, merciless drops. The dark forest loomed in her path, full of demons and ghosts of poor, starving peasants. She had never thought to be one of them. Where could she find shelter on this godforsaken night? She walked on, wet, cold, weary, feeling numb. She had already lived through the worst possible things. She had nothing left to love or fear.

The night grew very dark suddenly, as though a hand had painted a streak of black across the sky. A listlessness fell upon Jacqueline, and her strength ebbed. She sank to the ground, grasping the wet cloak tightly against the wind and rain.

Then despair washed over her. *I should let it take me,* she thought. *Am I going mad? Why not give up my life to this cold night?*

Blackness settled upon her, and consciousness dimmed. Then, through closed lids, she seemed to see a flicker of light. Awareness began to dawn. Her eyes opened.

The room around her was dim and poor but cheerful, lit with a single glowing candle. Something touched Jacqueline's brow that was cool and soothing.

"Dearie," muttered a low voice.

Mother! Thought Jacqueline in a burst of emotion. Then her eyes focused on a rather plump, doughy face encased in a kerchief. The face seemed lit with kindness. The woman's hand touched her forehead, and calmness descended upon Jacqueline.

"We found you in the forest, child. Poor dear, so chill and wet. My husband, he is a kind man. He carried you here. Now drink this, lass, you will feel stronger."

A cup of warm mead was lifted to her lips. She sipped, choked, then swallowed most of the contents. Its warmth flowed through her veins.

"Thank you," she said, with an effort. "How kind."

"But why is such a little lass out alone on this ungodly night? Are you lost, child?"

"Yes," Jacqueline said bitterly. "Yes, I am lost."

She must have slept again then, for she remembered no more of this conversation. In the morning the woman came to her with a meager meal, her plump face glowing. Jacqueline could hardly bear her kindness. *If only she knew the things I have done, would she be so kind,* she wondered.

"You are welcome to stay, child," said the woman. "I am Mistress Fletcher. My husband and I are poor, but we are willing to share." A shadow passed over the broad face. "We lost our own child, years ago. She would have been about your age now."

"I am sorry," Jacqueline said. Her voice sounded strange to her ears. She thought she had forgotten how to speak. "I cannot stay. But..." her voice almost broke and she caught herself. "I appreciate your kindness."

"Child," said the woman. She was not one to ask questions or intrude, but this pale girl looked so young and so forlorn, as though she had gone through a terrible ordeal. "It is nothing to me, I know. But my husband found you, cold and wet and ill, and we feel responsible. You told me that you are lost. Have you no one to care for you, no family? It is not seemly for a young girl to be traveling alone.."

"No!" Jacqueline broke in harshly, then went on in a softer tone, "I have no family. I have no one to go back to."

The woman was a peasant, uneducated, but she was perceptive. She read the secret pain in the girl's voice and knew this was something that must not be pursued, for it would cost the girl dear to speak of it.

"There, child. I did not mean to pry. Only tell me when you wish to leave here so that I may fix you some food to take with you."

Jacqueline bowed her head in gratitude. "Tomorrow, I think. I will feel well enough and I cannot accept your kind charity any longer. I will go tomorrow."

The woman nodded and asked no more questions.

But the next day Jacqueline was too ill to move. The woman found her in the morning covered with sweat, breathing heavily, unconscious.

"The plague!" breathed her husband and crossed himself.

"Nay," said his wife. "This is not the plague. This poor girl has suffered some tragedy she cannot bear. There is war within her soul and it causes her body to fall sick."

The man looked intently at his wife and believed her, for she was a wise woman, and knew much of illness and ways to heal it.

"I shall go to the fields then, and leave her to your good care, wife."

He came to her and kissed her cheek, looking down at Jacqueline. "Poor lass," he sighed, for he was a kind-hearted man, and adored young people. "Is there anything you need, my dear?"

"Yes, if you will get me some feverfew, it will cool her fever."

In the dark of her illness Jacqueline's mind drifted and left her. It seemed to float in space and time, sending back images to her sleeping brain. In sleep time –passing did not exist. All times existed at once. It was before Guillaume's death, it was after. It was all one.

So the images came, not as they had happened in time, one after the other, but in brief electric moments, all mixed up. In the dream his death passed before her inner eyes, then lifted like a black cloud and he lived again, touching her hand, smiling. His green eyes were entities in themselves, alive; they seemed to exist without him, suspended in space, creating a warmth that enveloped her.

Jacqueline's mind could no longer accept his image, dead. Her mind infused him with life, making him rise, making him move and eat and speak. She had seen him once, just after death, but her mind covered that image with his living self. In sleep she did not have to remember the emptiness which was hers upon waking.

But waking comes and with it comes the other reality.

The woman watched Jacqueline in her pain. She could see the torment in the girl's restless movements on the bed. She could hear the tortured words, and something that sounded like a name- Guillaume. It fell from her lips again and again. Then a soft look would come over her face, a look of love. *Her lover,* the woman thought. Even as she watched, Jacqueline's features twisted in a spasm of pain. "No!" the word came from her lips a shriek, a cry of pure horror. The woman started and took the girl's clammy hand. *What had happened to this child,* she thought fiercely, protectively. *What had been done to her?*

She soothed the girl with cool, wet cloths and Jacqueline quieted. And when she was quieter, the woman went to the corner of her poor hovel, knelt before the wooden cross her husband had made, and prayed for the girl's tortured soul.

Chapter 26

When Jacqueline at last awakened to consciousness she did not recall the tortured dreams of her long sleep, nor did she know how long she had been ill. She only felt that she had been through yet another ordeal, and a great weariness was in her soul. But though the soul was not so easily healed, the body was, with Mistress Fletcher's good nursing. Jacqueline ate the simple but good food, drank the warming broths, and felt strength ebb back into her thin form. When she felt better, she knew she must go.

When she spoke to the old couple of leaving they urged her to stay. "You can live with us, child," said Mistress Fletcher, her husband nodding agreement. "We lost our own child long ago. We would be glad to have you stay." But Jacqueline knew that such a life was not meant for her. She needed to find something; she knew not what. But though there was love in this poor hovel, she was not ready to accept it. She declined their offer and told them that it could not be, though she thanked them with all her heart. She tried to give them a little money, knowing their poverty, but they were offended, saying they did not help her for gain, but out of Christian charity. Jacqueline felt humbled by their goodness.

In the end she made them a present of some cloth she had brought with her. It was coarse cloth, but since it was a gift freely given, they accepted it happily, knowing it meant something to Jacqueline to be able to give it. They told her of some people they knew in a nearby town, knowing that she had no place to go. "Go to Master le Mire. He runs an inn and perhaps he can give you work." But she refused this too, knowing that whatever she did next must be of her own finding.

So early one morning, goodbyes said, she walked out the door and set her foot again on the path through the woods. She walked on, and when she could no longer walk, she stopped to rest on the cool forest grass. She ate the food Mistress Fletcher had prepared for her. Her mind was a fog, she thought of nothing. She moved as though in a dream. She did not think of Guillaume.

I remember that time even now as if it had been a dream, the old nun thought. *Or a nightmare.* To move through life in such a haze had a nightmarish quality, as though there were no mind inhabiting the weary body. *My mind was elsewhere, in some other place and time,* she thought. It could not remain in the present, for the present without Guillaume was too painful. Perhaps that was why it had happened. She had thought at first that a devil's madness had come over her. But now, pondering, gazing out her window at the spreading dusk after Compline, she wondered whether that strange vision too had been given by God.

Jacqueline had been weary, having slept by the roadside the night before. She had risen in the morning with vague, uncertain steps, eating the good food Mistress Fletcher had given her to give her the strength to move on. The day was hazy, promising some warmth before the noon. As she walked she came out of the forest, and the fields spread out around her, rich with the green of spring. The dusty road stretched out before her, seeming endless. She did not know where it led. In the distance she could see the peasants who worked the fields pulling their carts, planting seeds that would flourish in the fullness of summer. She could hear their voices in the distance, drifting toward her on the heavy air.

Then suddenly the scene around her seemed to fade and shift. She heard voices, but they were no longer the voices of the peasants. She heard a woman's voice shouting something in an unfamiliar tongue. She heard a loud noise that startled her, a nose unlike any that she had ever heard before, like the rumbling of a cart, but magnified many times over. She saw a road, but it was not the dusty road she had been walking. It was very wide and of a cold gray color. Then the picture altered again, changing back to the original scene, the dusty road, the brown fields. The sounds of the peasant's voices came back to her. Jacqueline's heart was beating very fast. She stopped and sat down, trying to calm her confused mind. *Am I going mad?* She thought. *Is the devil plaguing me?*

Soon she moved on, for there was nothing else to do. But she did not forget, and she was stirred out of her utter lethargy. The vision had been fearful, not bringing any of the peace and joy that the first vision in the wood had brought on that long-ago day. After awhile Jacqueline thought of the strange scene as a temporary madness, arising from her confused and dreamlike state.

But now, over the years, the old nun knew better. She was not certain what she had seen, but she knew that it was given to her to see what others could not. And she had learned that there were occasions when time was not a flowing thing but bent and twisted and became warped. There were instances in a lifetime when one stands on the brink of the world and looks beyond. Not all can do this, and the old nun no longer had visions. But her younger self had. As she grew older, she had learned to see it as a gift, and to thank God for it, though it puzzled her. Seeing the frightening vision that day had in a way been a good thing, for it stirred her emotions, drawn her out of her vagueness. And in the end, she had come to believe, the strange visions had played a part in bringing her to her purpose, the purpose that had led to the tragedy and had set her feet upon that dusty road. She had achieved her purpose in the end.

The old nun smiled. Still, that fact brought her joy. After all that had happened, God had accepted her as one of his own.

Chapter 27

Jacqueline had walked all day, then when her legs could move no more, she collapsed, and lay where she fell, falling into a fitful sleep.

She opened her eyes, but for a moment thought she was still dreaming for the face floating above her was twisted, leering, the stuff of nightmares. Then the face spoke, and Jacqueline started sharply, feeling a stab of fear.

"A girl," the face said, moving back. It was a man, very poorly dressed, his face dirty, beard ragged. His mouth was twisted to one side by a deep scar. "A comely wench, I vow, beneath the clothes."

Jacqueline heard his words through a mist, and the irony of the situation smote her; that she, nobly born, should be on a dusty road in dirty clothes, bantered over by this piece of filth. Her instinct for self-preservation, that she had thought lost, came back to her despite her fear.

The man came closer and she could see his companion, an equally filthy boy of about fifeen. The boy held a knife, and the blade glittered in the early slanting sunlight.

"And, I vow, this one's for free!" he said, smacking his lips. The man laughed, and reached down to fumble at her dress. A vivid image tore Jacqueline's brain, a painful image of Guillaume as her lover, touching her with gentle passion...

"Do not touch me," she said. Her voice was low and cool. "I am dedicated to God. I am traveling to my convent, where I am to become a nun."

The man hesitated.

"If you touch me, God will surely punish you."

The boy lowered his knife. His face showed fear. The man still clutched at the cloth of her dress, but the boy said, "Nay, leave her be. If she speaks true we will be sore punished."

"She is no nun," the man said, though doubt shone in his face.

"But I am promised," Jacqueline said, still calm.

"Leave her be," the boy said again. "I know of a man who took a nun- he was struck by lightning next day. Leave her. There be other wenches."

The man moved away from Jacqueline and both fled through the trees.

Jacqueline sat for a long while, trying to calm her wildly beating heart.

The lie she had told was foul blasphemy, but it had saved her. Though she was no maid, she had chosen Guillaume out of love. Her betraying body was still her own. It would have been a desecration to let that filth touch her, so soon after Guillaume.... But she had come very close. Perhaps it had been folly not to take the Fletcher's advice, and to go to their friend. What did she know of a vagabond's life? Yet it was her life now. She was alone, and she must go on alone.

As she rose, something glittered in the dust at her feet. She bent to examine it- it was the knife. The boy had dropped it when he ran off. She hesitated but a moment. Then she picked it up, put it in her girdle, and walked on.

The knife made Jacqueline feel safer somehow. She walked with a more certain step. As twilight came again, she settled under a tree, drew her cloak around her, and clutched the knife in her hand.

Jacqueline woke with a start and felt a stab of fear. What had wakened her? More ragged men with evil on their minds? She listened intently, but heard no sound. The moon had come up, and she could see the shadows of the trees around her, nothing more.

The moon. She gazed at it, remembering the night of the full moon when Guillaume had come to her. What different circumstances than now, alone in a vast forest, Guillaume forever lost to her. It seemed so long ago, it seemed lifetimes ago.

The stars were out and her eyes roamed over the patterns they made in the sky. They were so ordered, so perfect there, unchanging, pure. What were they? What were they made of?

A sudden intensity grasped Jacqueline, a feeling that the stars were real, alive, and watching over her, smiling down at her. She felt their presence and a sense of peace settled into her heart. Is heaven up there somewhere? She had always had an image of it, gold-paved streets and angels singing. But what was it really? For the first time she saw how small had been her concept of heaven. For the truth was far greater than anything her merely human mind could conceive of. The thought for some reason comforted her. There had to be a pattern in the world. And Guillaume...he must live, he must exist somewhere....

As she had that thought, she heard a rustling in the trees behind her. And she did not fear, for she sensed Guillaume, felt his presence through her very pores. She did not turn. She knew it would not be his physical form there, the Guillaume she had known. But he was, he existed...the green eyes were closed, but the bright spirit was somewhere... She slept then, with the peace of knowing.

The old nun remembered, in the half-waking moments of pre-dawn, before Vespers. She had never felt Guillaume's presence again so strongly, but the feeling had come when she most sorely needed reassurance. He had come to her again, in her great need. Somehow, wherever he was, his spirit knew, and communed with her troubled spirit. He had truly loved her. The old nun sighed. How many secrets were shrouded in time's misty fog? Only for brief moments does there come a gap in the dimension; the fog rolls away and reveals something, just for an instant, then swirls back again and the gap is closed. But once you have bridged that gap, however briefly, you are always aware of the simple truth; there is something more than just this world we see. That night, when Guillaume came to her in spirit, the gap was bridged.

The next morning Jacqueline had risen, feeling Guillaume's spirit to be still with her. He stayed throughout the morning. His memory clung like a comforting cloak. As the day wore on, however, realism took his place. Jacqueline was hungry and tired. A weakness fell upon her, and she feared illness again. But there was no place to go and nothing to eat. She could only trudge on.

At last she saw the buildings of a town in the distance. A town meant a marketplace and food to eat, for she had money left to buy. The sight gave her renewed hope and energy, and she traversed the distance quickly.

She made her way through the crowded marketplace, only half-aware of the noise and movement around her. People shouted, greeting friends, calling out their wares. They were soil-stained, hard-working peasants, in town for market day. She could walk among them unnoticed; she was one of them now, in her old brown wool housedress and soiled cloak.

Jacqueline bought bread and a slice of cheese, obtained some water from a girl who was selling cloth, and settled near a pile of hay to eat the first food she'd had since early the previous day. She, who had dined on red meat and wine and fish and pastries, all in one day, was learning to live with hunger. It was only a pang of the stomach, soon stilled. The pangs of the soul went deeper, mattered much more.

She ate quickly, crudely, as she had learned to do. It did not matter anymore; it was so easy to slip out of the habit of manners. When finished, she wiped her fingers on her skirt and looked around, really noticing the scene for the first time.

The faces struck her eye, the sea of faces. At first they all looked alike, as like as stalks of hay swaying in the wind. Then some altered, standing out in the sea, giving evidence of the person within. She saw a round-faced old woman, kindly, so like Mistress Fletcher that for a moment Jacqueline thought it was her. But no, only another of her kind, of the thousands of nameless women who live obscure lives and die and give so much to those who need them. She saw a man, middle-aged, red-faced, arguing loudly with a young woman whose face was equally red with anger. She saw an old man, sitting near his cart of wares, sitting very still, the lines of his face engraved so deeply they were like works of art, sketched in a fine hand. There were children too, running about in the melee, some rosy-cheeked and happy, like Cecile had been, some fragile, drawn, looking much older than their years.

These are the people who work my father's lands, Jacqueline thought, *those who work so hard, and for almost nothing. I am one of them now.* They lived to survive, going from day to day, not knowing what the future would bring, not even knowing for sure whether it would come at all. Now she too lived just to survive. She did not think about surviving; she did it, and thought about nothing. Or perhaps it was not that she thought about nothing. Perhaps the thoughts came so fast, crowding her consciousness until their edges blurred, that she could not tell one thought from the other, so they seemed like no thoughts at all. It was far better to empty her brain, to involve herself in other people's faces, to let their beings, their noisy dirty selves, as open and spontaneous as animals, to crowd her mind. She could simply experience them and forget all else, until the moment came to eat or sleep again.

In the corner of her eye, Jacqueline caught a movement near her, a blur of grey. She turned. A child came closer, a child with tangled filthy hair, a dirty face and ragged clothes. The child held out a hand. It was missing two fingers.

"Alms," the child whined. Jacqueline drew back instinctively. Images flooded her brain, images of the young Ralf and Cecile, so round and pretty, then, an image of Robert as a rosy-cheeked baby. She gazed into the empty eyes of the hungry child and saw Robert's dark eyes. Pity for the child stirred within her. She leaned forward.

"What is your name?" she asked gently.

"Name. Name." the child repeated blankly. *My God,* she thought. *How much worse this child's life has been than mine ever was.*

Though that thought did not take away the pain and emptiness of her present being, it did fill Jacqueline with action. She must do something to help this child. The idea had great immediacy. She was unsure of what to do, but having taken care of her younger siblings, she knew that first the child must be fed. Her own meager meal was gone, and her money was dwindling, but she pulled a coin from her small sack and held out her hand. "Come with me," she said. The child gazed at her. "Come." She took the child's mutilated hand. The remaining small fingers closed around hers willingly enough.

"Come, come, come," the child chanted as they walked.

Jacqueline bought a small loaf at a booth, giving it to the child, who consumed it like a starving animal, with low grunts and fearful eyes, as though someone would come and snatch the food away.

The woman who had sold her the loaf gazed with disgust at the child, then turned to Jacqueline.

"What are you doing with him, Mistress? Look how dirty he is."

"He was hungry."

"We have all been hungry at one time or another. At least my man and I work for our food. So do our children. This one…" She spat into the ground in distaste…"Is the child of the beggars, who live off hard-working folk like us, and breed more filthy beggars. "

"What about his hand?" Jacqueline asked in a low voice, so the child could not hear.

"They did it. His people. They cut off his fingers. If the child lives, he makes a more pathetic sight, all mutilated. It gets more money."

"They do it…" Jacqueline felt a sickness in the pit of her stomach.

"Best leave him be. They'll be angry if he comes back with no money and they'll beat him."

"No, they won't. I will take him with me."

"Take him!" The woman laughed a humorless laugh. "Why, in God's name would you do that?"

Why? Because the child was lost, as lost as she. Because he needed her. Or perhaps she needed him more than he needed her. Why?

Jacqueline took the child's hand and walked away without answering.

Chapter 28

Jacqueline was wandering in a vast tangled forest. She had lost her child and she was calling him, calling…But now she could no longer call him, she could not remember his name. What was his name? She could not remember his name, but she could see his eyes, large and round and dark like Robert's…

Jacqueline opened her eyes, startled. An edge of haze spread over the distant hills, widening into bands of pink. She was huddled near a wall at the edge of town. Something moved nearby, and her mind jerked awake. The child.

He had not yet spoken anything meaningful, except for the word "alms," and this he had ceased to say. His mouth worked, but without sound. He crawled toward her and grabbed mutely at her cloak, stuffing its edge into his mouth. She pulled it away and a low moan burst from him. He did not scream or cry, only moaned, and rocked back and forth on his haunches.

"Here," she said quickly, thrusting some bread into his hands. As he ate, she poured water into her mug and gave it to him. She sat back to watch him eat. His pupils grew large and black at the sight of food, and he immersed himself in his meal; while he ate, there was only the food and his satisfied belly. It was enough for him. He lived to eat.

And she? Was she truly one such as him? Could she continue to live such a life, continue it until she died?

Jacqueline could not answer those questions yet. She stored them away in her mind. But one question was immediate and must be answered. What should she do with this child?

He had finished eating and was staring at her blankly, as though he could look right through her eyes. Again she felt time hurtling back, and saw her brother Robert before her, his dark eyes laughing at some new game they played. How long ago had Robert died? Her first and last tears.

She tugged her mind back to the present. She looked and saw the child as he was, not the brother that she had lost, but a tattered mindless beggar child.

"You must have parents," she said, and thought as she said it, but I do not. "Where is your mama?"

The first emotion she had seen in him leapt into his eyes. Fear. He began to gabble, sounds she could not understand.

"No," she said. "Never mind." He still looked at her with fear, not understanding.

She did not want to touch him, to comfort him. The touch of another human body would be too painful. She did not want to...

She leaned forward, reaching out, her arm encircled his frail shoulders, pulling him closer. He relaxed, stopped shaking and gabbling. After a moment he put his thumb in his mouth and sucked it loudly.

Jacqueline could not relax with the child against her. She could feel his aliveness, the throb of his pulse, his warm humanity, and could hardly bear it. The memory was too recent, too sharp. The last time she had felt such close human touch it had been Guillaume's. Guillaume...Then the intensity of the pain began to numb her. She sat very still, letting numbness comfort her.

The child slept awhile and after the sleep, his fear was gone. He awoke thinking only of food again. Jacqueline had none left, and she too was hungry. She rose, the child with her, and they started toward the marketplace. The child clung to her skirt as they walked among the crowd, as though he feared to lose her. He had come to trust her. She was his lifeline now. And in a way, he was hers, for what other reason did she have to live?

A man watched them, unseen. He saw Jacqueline go to the well and draw water, first for the boy, and then herself. He saw her buy bread and cheese and watched the two eat it quickly as they stood. Her son? the man asked himself, but then decided no, she was too young. Her brother then? But no...

The man moved through the crowd to get a little closer. He saw the blank look in the child's eyes as he neared, saw his tattered clothes. He saw the girl, in a dirty wool dress and cloak, her hood flung carelessly over her dark brown rippling hair. Her features were strongly molded, but he could not see her eyes. They were downcast as she ate.

She finished, licking her fingers, then looked up and met the man's gaze. He was taken aback at the pain in her eyes, a deep still pain that seemed to have settled permanently into the dark depths. So- he had been right then.

Seeing this man, Jacqueline took the child's hand and walked through the crowd in the opposite direction. She could not speak to one such as he. She could not bear the compassion in his eyes, she must run from that compassion, far from anything to do with the church. For he, in his monk's garb, reminded her too strongly of her lost dream.

Chapter 29

The monk could not see her as she became lost in the crowd but her image stayed in his mind. It was not only her noble bearing, incongruous with the dirty clothes and the thin form that spoke of hunger, not only the pain in her eyes that drew him to her. He thought he knew who she was. There were mutterings about the cast-off daughter of Lord Bonel, a nobleman of Suffolk. But how he knew that this dirty peasant girl was that daughter he could not say. He simply knew, knowing with his heart, not his mind. He had to help her. He could see her terrible yearning, though she blocked it from herself. He had to help her, but he must never let her know what he knew about her.

Of all that had happened since her banishment, Jacqueline feared the monk most. He had seen her, she knew, seen her inner self, her pain. And he was a symbol of all she had given up. She could not bear that he saw through the hard shell she had grown. She must not allow him to see her again.

Jacqueline thought of leaving the town, but what of the child? She could not take him on the road. He was weak and always hungry, and he would slow her down. And neither could she leave him. He was bound to her somehow. His trust was a chain, but she could not break it. She would not do to this child what had been done to her.

The child seemed content now. He sat on the ground near her, babbling to himself, sucking on his stunted fingers. A feeling of hopelessness overwhelmed her. She could go on like this for only a few more weeks. Her money was fast running out, with both herself and the child to feed. She could not work; she knew nothing about finding work. She was lost and she needed help. Unbidden, the thought of the monk's kind eyes rose in her mind.

But in the next instant she pushed it away. She could ask no one for help. This was her punishment and she must endure it alone.

The next morning Jacqueline took the child and went a short way into the wood to look for berries. It would be cheaper to forage for food if she could than to buy it for herself and the boy too. He was attached to her now, very strongly. Wherever she went, he followed, like an animal responding to the one who feeds it. They found some wild strawberries and ate their fill. Then Jacqueline sat down, plucking at pine needles, trying to plan. She could not stay, but neither could she go. Perhaps she could ask for some type of work. She knew how to keep house, how to sew; perhaps that knowledge would be of value to someone.

The child whimpered and plucked at Jacqueline's dress. She got up. He took her hand and they started walking down the forest path. It was the first time he had taken any such initiative. Curious, she followed where he led.

After awhile, Jacqueline was startled to see a small building in a clearing. Moving closer, she saw it was a church. Involuntarily she gasped and stopped short. She had not been inside a church since before…It had been so long. She must not defile a church by going inside. She was too great a sinner.

Yet her feet moved, following the child who babbled excitedly, pulling her forward.

The door creaked open. The inside of the small chapel was filled with voices raised in song. Grey-hooded monks, their faces hidden, walked down the aisle holding tall tapers. They did not appear to see her and the boy. The child, his babbling hushed, stood still by her side.

Jacqueline blinked and swayed. The church was empty. The altar was dusty and plain, the stone walls bare. Empty. There were no monks, no chanting; it was empty and totally still. But what had she just seen?

Again, again had come the strange lapse of time and space. If not for the boy, Jacqueline would have thought she was going mad. But he had seen the vision too. He stood beside her now, his eyes wide and staring, uncomprehending. And she understood as little as he.

Even now, thought the old nun, *even now with the wisdom of my long years I do not understand those visions. I have only learned to accept, not to understand. Yet somehow those visions played vital parts in my life, led me down paths I would not otherwise not have trod.*

Shaken by the experience in the chapel in the wood, Jacqueline made her way to a stone bench along the wall and sat down heavily. The child followed her closely. And the urge came upon her, overwhelming her- the urge to pray, to ask forgiveness, to begin again. Yet she could not. She was unworthy of forgiveness.

The voice stunned her, making her jump.

"Only God can judge you," it said. "Do not try to judge yourself."

Jacqueline turned toward the voice and saw the brown eyes of the monk whom she had seen in town and run away from. She did not ask him how he had read her thoughts. Anything seemed possible in this place of visions. Perhaps he too was not real.

But he was real. Jacqueline saw that as he approached her. There were deep lines around his warn dark eyes, and his hands were veined and work-worn. She could not tell his age. He looked kind. Even the child, usually so fearful, did not shirk, but went up and touched the monk's rough brown robe as he sat down near them.

"How did you know I was here?" Jacqueline asked, for she knew he had not found her by chance.

"They all come here. All those who are weary and in pain, those who are needful." She looked at him sharply. "Sometimes," he continued softly, touching the boy's head, "a child brings them. Children know this place is special, though they are not aware that they know." The monk looked around the old church. "They say a miracle happened here one hundred years ago. There was a child, very sick. His mother, troubled, brought her son to this old church and asked the monks to help her. He was her only child and her husband had been killed in a battle.

"So the monks took pity on this good woman. They all gathered together in this little church and a mass was said, while the sick boy lay near the altar with his mother holding him. And, as the holy Eucharist was given out, the boy opened his eyes and raised his head, and the mother knew that he would live. And it is said that whenever a troubled soul comes here, the monks pray again."

"Yes," Jacqueline said slowly, in wonder. "I saw them. We both saw them."

"It is a sign of hope, child," the monk said softly. "All do not see them."

"Hope," she said. Could there ever be hope for her again? Perhaps. Yet she still did not know where to go, or how she and the child would live.

"You must be hungry, child. Come with me and I will give you some food."

"And him?" she said quickly, pointing to the boy.

"Of course. He is yours, I can see."

"Oh, no, he is not mine…" she began, but the monk cut her off.

"Yes, he is yours. He is your child of the heart. He is very much like you. And he loves you more than he has ever loved anyone." The monk smiled and his smile was like a sunrise. "You have saved him."

I, she thought. *I, who am so lost, how could I have saved this beggar-child? He still does not speak. He seems so mindless.* And yet, as she looked at him, the boy caught her eye and grinned, and took her hand in his own. Her heart jumped in a kind of pain. She had not even noticed this poor child's love. But it was there.

"Come," the monk said, rising. "We shall eat." He turned and looked into Jacqueline's eyes. "I am Brother Giles."

Chapter 30

Jacqueline, Brother Giles and the child made their way through the woods back to the town, and to an old comfortable looking building located next to a church. Jacqueline shrank a bit, but Brother Giles touched her shoulder gently. "I am taking you to Father Flaubert. This is his parish. His housekeeper will give you food and there is a room for pilgrims where you can stay. For you too are a pilgrim, child."

Jacqueline looked into his warm eyes and could not help but believe him. She said, "What of the boy?"

"He shall stay with you."

"Brother," she spoke hesitantly, not wanting to depend on this man's kindness. "What then? I cannot live on charity."

"Give him a name," came the strange answer.

"What?"

"Give the boy a name. Did not Jesus say that the birds of the air need not worry, for the heavenly father feeds them? Trust in this, child. That is why we monks and priests are here; to aid those in need. Just as you are helping this boy. We will speak of the future later, when you are better able. For now, give the boy a name. He needs a name."

Jacqueline looked at the child. Somehow he seemed changed since the vision in the church. His face was calmer, he seemed more normal. He looked peaceful, almost happy, no longer the gibbering beggar boy.

"What shall I call you?" she said to him softly, bending down to his height. He gazed at her steadfastly. Painfully she thought of Guillaume. But no, she could not speak his name; she could not give his name away. It belonged to him alone.

Then a thought came to mind. "Gabriel." Without her being fully conscious of the idea, the name rolled off her tongue.

"It is a good name. 'Man of God.' A good name," said Brother Giles.

"Do you like it?" Jacqueline said, speaking softly, face to face with the child. "Gabriel?" He looked at her and his lips moved.

"Say it," she instructed. "Ga-bri-el."

"Ga…"

"Ga-bri-el." She wanted so much for him to understand.

"Ga-beel."

"Yes!" Jacqueline cried, smiling, lost in the child's success. He was glowing at the pleasure he had given her.

"Gabeel," he repeated.

"That is you. That is your name. Gabriel." Then she looked at Brother Giles.

"See what a gift you have given him?" he said. She nodded. It was true. Sinner that she was, lost as she felt, she had still given hope to this child.

"And now," said Brother Giles, "What is your name?"

Suddenly she knew fear again. She did not want to let him know. She feared that word had spread of her father's deed. She wanted no one to connect her with the past. Yet, this kind monk who had given her so much- perhaps she could trust him. She had to trust in order to survive. It was unlikely that he, a monk of a poor order, would have heard the news of young Lady Bonel's disgrace and banishment.

"Jacqueline."

"A pretty name." No strange reaction crossed his face, no dawning of recognition. "Come. I will introduce you to Father Flaubert and Mistress Leroy, his housekeeper."

Mistress Leroy met them at the door. She was a plump quiet woman who radiated peace. Brother Giles greeted her, then explained that Jacqueline and Gabriel needed food and a place to stay.

"Yes, of course," said Mistress Leroy, as though it were a request made of her every day. "Come. I will show you to your room and soon supper will be ready." They submitted to her capable hands.

Father Flaubert was at supper when they came down. He was a tall, slender man with deep sunken cheeks and grave eyes. Jacqueline's heart jumped in fear at the sight of him. But as she and Gabriel entered the room he rose, extended his hand, and smiled with singular sweetness.

"You are very welcome here," he said, and his voice was rich and vibrant with good will. Here was a man who truly loved his fellow humans, and who took great pleasure in their company. He set Jacqueline further at ease by not asking about her at all, but telling them stories about the town and the townspeople, and parish work, light-hearted tales that gave no threat.

After supper, Brother Giles, who had stayed to eat with them, departed, saying to Jacqueline that he would return the next day to discuss Gabriel.

That night Jacqueline and the boy slept side by side on a soft comfortable pallet. For once, the demons of sleep did not disturb her mind.

Chapter 31

For a week, little happened. Jacqueline fell into the routine of helping Mistress Leroy with household tasks. She had been running a large household for so long that she worked effortlessly in this small one. Mistress Leroy commented on her capability, but said nothing more. No questions were asked.

Jacqueline felt some guilt at living on charity. Her family had been of the proud nobility and now she had nothing, and must depend on strangers. She felt tempted to confess the terrible sin that had led to her banishment to Father Flaubert, to ease her mind's burden, yet she did not. They did not ask about her past, how she had come to be there, and she did not tell. Neither did Brother Giles, though he knew.

For those days, after chores were done in the morning, Jacqueline was much involved with Gabriel. He seemed happy living in the parish house, and Mistress Leroy and Father Flaubert were kind and patient with him. He had lost his aura of desperation and behaved in a calmer manner, as though he realized he would not be alone and hungry any longer. His love for Jacqueline was more and more apparent, making her feel unworthy. But she was growing to love him too, and the emotion was painful. She had so suddenly lost all she ever loved that she was afraid to risk love again.

In those long afternoons Jacqueline sat with the boy, and tried to teach him. She said his name over and over, and he would repeat it until he could speak it faultlessly, and associate it with himself. He would come running joyfully when someone called out for him. She taught him to say "food" and "sleep." Then she tried teaching him her name. It was difficult for him to say, and he stumbled, but he tried very hard to please her. She also taught him simple chores that he could do with his stunted fingers. And while she did all this, she waited, for she knew that this good and simple life could not last. All of her questions about the future were still there.

Then Brother Giles came, as he said he would.

He and Jacqueline were shown into a small side room by Mistress Leroy, and left alone. Brother Giles remained silent for awhile, and Jacqueline's nervousness grew. Finally she burst out, "Well? What is to become of me?"

Brother Giles gazed at her for a long moment before replying. "That," he said, "is up to you."

"But I do not know!"

"It will come to you."

He was not going to give her easy answers, she realized. Perhaps it was best. But there was one very large question that he could help her answer.

"You said you would help me. I need your help with Gabriel. I cannot keep him. I am poor, I have no home. I cannot give him any sort of life."

"Yes. That is why I am here. I have spoken to the brothers at the monastery. My superiors are agreeable. We are a poor order, and we farm for our living. But we also have a tradition of learning and knowledge. For hundreds of years we have run schools for the poor boys of the district. We teach them, and they work with us. When they are older, they are free to leave or to take their vows."

"And?" she asked, her heart pounding.

"We will take Gabriel, if you give your permission."

"Brother Giles, I thank you so much. But you know, as I do that…well, he is feeble-minded."

Brother Giles smiled and said softly, "Sometimes, Jacqueline, we can learn more from the simple-minded than they can learn from us. Gabriel is close to life, close to his feelings. When he loves, he loves completely. He is closer to God than you or I."

"Surely closer to God than I, for I am far away from God," she said, so softly she wasn't sure he had heard.

But he had. "Maybe you will tell me when you trust me, child. But if you do not choose to tell me, do not hesitate to tell God of your pain. He will listen. And, child, if you feel he does not answer right away, do not despair. The answer will come."

Jacqueline bowed her head, ashamed. He had seen right into her heart. He knew her guilt.

Brother Giles rose. "Goodbye, Jacqueline. Talk to Gabriel. I will return tomorrow. We can bring him to the monastery then, if that is what you decide to do."

"Goodbye," she said softly, not meeting his eyes. But she could not get his words out of her mind. This kind and wise man saw good in her. The thought awed her. If he only knew what she had done. And that she had forsaken God. Yet…could he be right? For a brief moment, she permitted herself to hope. She was young, she had done penance. Could she be forgiven and face life anew?

Guillaume's face floated before her, blocking her hope with a shadow of pain. How could God forgive me? How could Guillaume forgive me? Look what my love brought him to. She shook her head slowly. It could not be. The burden would be hers forever. But there was, at least, one thing she could do. She could save Gabriel.

The old nun sighed, peering out the tower window. It was tiring to be old. Sometimes she wanted to laugh and sing, to dance, to run through the tall summer grass. Her youth had been so bereft of such pleasures, and now her age made her too infirm. But she still had the gift of sight, and she could see the enormous beauty of God's handiwork. The sun slanted low over the distant hills, diffusing the world with a golden flush. She felt the sun on her face and her hands, turning her own wrinkled skin into gold. It was her gift that after long years of despair, of praying for forgiveness, of penance, she had found hope again. It was her gift that she could take pleasure in the small things in life; the song of the birds, the sunlight on her skin. Tonight it was too beautiful to think. There were times when she needed to contemplate her past, to investigate her inner being, to be the person God meant her to be. And there were times when she must enjoy the fact that she was alive, and it was a sweet, warm summer's evening. She leaned upon the open window, smiling.

Brother Giles had returned the next day, as he had promised. Jacqueline's decision was made. "I would like Gabriel to go with you," she told him. Brother Giles nodded in silent approval.

"I have obtained permission to allow you to visit the monastery. Of course, there are places a woman cannot go, but I can show you our church and our gardens. We can talk further." His eyes probed hers. She looked away. "Yes," she said shortly, shaking off the feeling that he knew more of her soul than he revealed.

Jacqueline fetched Gabriel, and they set out. Brother Giles talked quietly to the boy about his new life. Gabriel did not appear to understand, but seemed content to walk between the two people in the world that he loved.

The buildings of the little monastery were old, crude and poor, but the farmlands and the vineyards were well kept. The land spread out, rich with the harvest. Jacqueline thought of her father's lands, the fields and woods where she had once walked. She pushed away the memory, and looked at Gabriel to see his reaction. He was quiet, but gazed intently at everything. Though he had no real language, he had a kind of animal wisdom. He knew instinctively that this visit was important to him.

"I know it looks poor," Brother Giles told Jacqueline, "But we are a loving community."

"I know," she said, "I can tell, for I have met you." She blushed, fearing herself too bold, but Brother Giles seemed touched. "Thank you, child," he said simply. He knew it was hard for her to reach out to another human being. But she was growing. He no longer feared for her soul. She was no longer in despair, though she herself did not recognize this truth yet.

They moved through the gate within the monastery walls, to the church. Brother Giles knelt and prayed, while Jacqueline stood stiffly, not knowing what to do. But then a strange thing happened. Gabriel went slowly forward, to the altar. He knelt next to Brother Giles, and looked at him expectantly. The monk moved the child's hands to make the sign of the cross, then murmured the Lord's prayer. Jacqueline stood watching, awed, as Gabriel tried haltingly to repeat the words.

Then the two arose, came to her, and together they stepped out of the small dim church into the sunshine. Brother Giles touched Gabriel's head. "He has come home, Jacqueline," he said. "Gabriel belongs here."

"Yes, yes, I see," she said slowly. "It is right that he should stay."

When the time came for Jacqueline to leave, Gabriel did not cling to her as he once would have. She knelt to face him and kissed him goodbye, her heart full. So many times she had not had the chance to say goodbye to one she loved. She murmured to him, told him she loved him, and it was as though she was telling all those others she had loved as well. And he smiled at her, and said in the same syllables, "Jacqueline." As she left she knew it was the right thing for him to stay. But now she was alone again.

The old nun laughed to herself as she watched the convent children running through the fields nearby. They clasped hands and swung around, then collapsed, laughing uproariously, into the tall grass. They were orphans, or virtual orphans, as Gabriel had been. She often wondered how he had fared in life. Had he ever learned to speak? But she felt a peace where he was concerned, for she knew she had served him well. She had fed him, loved him, and given him over to the care of someone more able than she; Brother Giles. Brother Giles. He was one of those who peopled her memory, his image as sharp as it was back in those troubled days. Though she had known him only a brief few weeks, he had taught her much. She realized this only later, when some semblance of peace had come to her; she realized then that he had held truth in his soul. He had tried to teach her the truth, and in doing so, had given her a richer gift than she had ever known. Deep in her heart, she thanked Brother Giles

Chapter 32

She was sinking in a deep dark sea. The waves were black, black as night. On a distant shore were people, warm houses and food, but the waves were sweeping her away. She awoke covered with sweat. Her mind formed a simple word, Guillaume. Guillaume, Guillaume. She spoke his name silently, screaming it in her brain. *I am alone again. Why did he leave me? Why did my father not let us be?*

Somehow Gabriel's company had numbed the anguish of her loss. Now it arose fresh, as though these months between had not passed at all. She thought of harming herself, as she had briefly before, but the idea that taking her own life would be a sin was too greatly imbued within her. Yet life was only a burden. All this time had passed, and she was still lost. Still lost. She buried her face in her hands. The pain was a black pain, too deep to bear. For there was not even God to turn to.

Brother Giles came to see her the next day. He looked at her gaunt face, her haunted eyes, and knew that some crisis had arisen in her soul. He said a quick silent prayer that he might be of help to her.

Jacqueline looked at him and through him. "Please go," she said in a hoarse whisper. "I cannot see you now."

Brother Giles stood steadfast, thinking of what to say, to do. Finally he spoke. "Love for the child, Gabriel, made you forget for awhile. Now he is gone from you, and the pain comes back. You have lost your dream."

She looked at him, amazed for a moment out of her despondency. *How much does he know?* She thought wildly, as she had wondered upon first meeting Brother Giles.

He came closer to her, his dark eyes boring into her. "You have lost your dream and cannot go on. You have lost everything. There is no reason to live. You call to God and there is no answer. You begin to doubt God's very existence. And yet, Jacqueline, the pain is still harder to bear because you were once joyous in life, and felt close to God. You have seen God manifest in his creations. You have had the grace to see what so few ever see. And now it is gone, and darkness has descended upon your soul."

The visions in the wood, she thought, *but how does he know? I did see such things, and they were shining...I was sure of my mission then....*

Jacqueline looked at Brother Giles. "How do you come to know so much of me?" She asked quietly. "Are you an angel, or a demon, that you see me so clearly?"

"No, Jacqueline. I am but a poor monk. But God has given me the grace to be very aware of people's sufferings. I see that you suffer deeply, child, and I know that you could not suffer so deeply had you not also known great joy. For the two go hand in hand, the capacity for joy and the capacity to suffer. And I know you have been close to God. All joy comes from God, no matter what sort it is. Just as all love comes from God."

His words were so full of meaning for her that they made her numb. She could not think of what it meant for her if they were true. Brother Giles saw the confusion, the questions in her eyes, and knew that now she must consult her own soul.

"Bless you, child," he said, making the sign of the cross over her head. "I will come again."

"All love comes from God…"

The words rang over and over in Jacqueline's brain, tolling like a constant bell amidst her confused thoughts. Surely not my love. It was a lustful sinful love. It was physical, not spiritual. And yet, were our spirits not bound together as one? But it did not make me think of God. It made me turn away from God, from religion, from my vocation…

"All love comes from God."

Oh, Brother Giles, it cannot be so, she thought. Then with all her heart she prayed to that God she could not believe in, "Let it be so, that my spirit and that of my beloved Guillaume's may be free!"

When Brother Giles came again to see her, her face was calmer, more at peace. She was willing to talk, though only a little at first.

"I wished," Jacqueline told him haltingly, "to become a nun." She looked into his eyes to see if there was surprise in them. There was none.

"Yes?" he said softly, urging her on.

"My father…" A shadow crossed her face. "My father wished me to marry." She fell silent for a few painful moments and he remained silent too. Since he knew who she really was, he knew the outline of her story. But he would never betray this knowledge to her, not even to help her. She must give the story of her own free will.

"But then," Jacqueline went on, her voice so low he had to strain to hear, "I made the acquaintance of the boy who groomed our horses."

Feeling overwhelmed her, and she clutched her hands to her chest. She must not betray the pain to Brother Giles. It belonged to her alone. She struggled to control the vivid pain. Guillaume's face seemed to float into her mind, his image so clear she almost cried out. And she said, "We fell in love."

It was said. Speaking the words brought back the stark reality of what she had lost. "I am not a maid," she whispered, telling of her final shame, waiting for his curse upon her. But he never gave it. She waited a time that seemed infinite, then looked up to meet his eyes. His gaze was steady, his brown eyes gentle. She became suddenly, unreasonably, angry.

"Why do you not tell me of my sin? Why do you not preach to me as you should? I have done wrong! What manner of holy man are you?" She stopped, biting her lip. All her life she had been taught to look up to those who had chosen the religious life, and she was yelling at this monk like a farmer's wife on market day. But his gaze did not change.

"Jacqueline," he said, "You want me to tell you that you have sinned. You want me to be shocked. You want to be punished. But... have you not already been punished?"

She paled. "How do you know?"

"I know that you have lost him that you loved. In some way you have lost him, or you would not be here. I also know, Jacqueline, that God does not consider it a sin to love."

"But love of this kind?" she said, feeling shamed to be telling him so much.

"Perhaps you should not have done it. I know the church fathers would say this. And I, who have taken a vow of chastity, should tell you this. But it was not a wanton act. You did love him, did you not?"

"Yes, I loved him," she said, her voice a whisper. "I did love him."

Brother Giles caught at her hands, which were twisting convulsively in her skirt.

"And what happened?" he asked softly.

"My father and brothers found us. They killed him." This she spoke dispassionately, for she could not speak it otherwise. She was holding herself in tight control. He could see the strain on her face.

"And so you left."

"I was sent away. But I would have left anyway. No," she corrected herself, "I would have let my father kill me too. But it was not to be."

"No, it was not to be. You are destined for something more."

Jacqueline looked up at him again, but could not manage to question him. She waited, not sure what she was waiting for. She longed for Guillaume so terribly. Her body and soul ached. She needed the balm of his warm green eyes, of his love for her. But that was not to be, it was never again to be. She closed her eyes in pain.

"You do not see it now, child," came the monk's soft voice, "but your suffering is not for naught. It serves some purpose. Perhaps someday you will look back and understand."

"No," she said, her eyes still full of pain, "This is a terrible thing. Why did I have to lose him?"

She is letting it out, Brother Giles thought. *She is releasing all the anguish that she has been holding inside. This is good that she should release all this pain.* He said a brief prayer of thanks that he should be the vessel of her release.

"I do not know why you had to lose him. Only God knows." Brother Giles answered Jacqueline's question.

"Why did he do this to us? Why could my sisters talk and dance openly with their young men and I had to slip away at night, to steal moments in the dirty stable to see him? Why did God take him?"

He thought she would cry then, but she did not. She turned on him fiercely.

"Tell me why!"

"I do not know," he repeated.

Her anger crumbled. "I cannot believe in God anymore," she said.

Brother Giles waited a long moment. Then he said very quietly, "Perhaps your old dream has been given back to you."

She raised her head to look at him, startled.

"Nay," she said, "You mock me."

"You know that I would not mock you, Jacqueline. You do not see clearly now. You see only evil. Your eyes are blind to good. Therefore you cannot see God and you say that he does not exist. But he does. This has happened for a purpose. But perhaps it is best not to question for now. You have much to do. You must regain your faith. You must regain possession of your soul."

"I am a great sinner," she said bitterly, bluntly.

"God forgives you, Jacqueline. It is you who cannot forgive yourself." He rose and left her without a goodbye.

I thought him cruel, the old nun thought. He told me things I was not ready to hear. I thought I was being humble, but in my arrogance I put myself above God. I enshrined my pain, I worshiped it. Brother Giles set me back on the path that day, though I did not quite realize it. He was my guide. She bowed her head and prayed, and there was quiet joy in her face.

Chapter 33

Jacqueline lifted the garment from the water, spread it on a rock, and squeezed the water out in quick, harsh movements. She was angry at Brother Giles, who told her what she did not want to hear, then left her to brood. He had not come for almost a week, and had sent no word. She was acting as a maidservant to Father Flaubert, but though it eased her guilt at living on his charity, it was not a role she cared for overmuch. Yet what else was there for her? All else had been lost. And she felt she could make no move until she consulted Brother Giles. Yet why should she feel such? What made him so important? She twisted the garment in her hand harder. Anger was better than the knowing pain of longing. She treasured her anger. She did not want to see Brother Giles again, yet she longed to see him. Still, he did not come. Finally she asked Father Flaubert to send for him. She feared he would demand to know why she would not talk to him of her troubles, since he was a priest, but he merely nodded, and agreed to have word sent. Brother Giles arrived the next day. She looked up from her stitching to see his straight brown-clothed figure coming up the path. She looked down quickly, concentrating on her work, to hide the eager gladness in her face.

He came up to where she sat. "Jacqueline," he said softly, in greeting.

"Why did you not come before?" she asked, then bit her lip. She had not meant to give herself away. But to her surprise, Brother Giles laughed.

"It was for you to send for me, child," he said. "I had no wish to force myself upon you, or to push you to accept the hard things you must learn. It had to be left up to you."

She gazed at him, then smiled too. "And so, I have sent for you," she said. "How is Gabriel?"

The monk's face softened. "He is well. He is truly God's child."

"Yes," Jacqueline murmured.

"So you have come to believe in God again," Brother Gile's voice came softly. Jacqueline looked at him in confusion.

"How can you say that Gabriel is God's child if there is no God?"

She caught his meaning and bowed her head. He caught her every slip, this man; he saw into her soul.

"I have lost him," she said, and Brother Giles was not sure whether she meant God or her lover.

"You have forsaken him," he answered her.

"No! He has forsaken me! Taken away my home, my family my lands and the one whom I loved above all!"

He wondered whether, in her anguish, she realized how much she had given away in speaking of her lands and her family. If he had been unaware of her identity, her outburst would have given him a clue.

"And perhaps he has given you something else, Jacqueline. Something to make the losing of all that you love have meaning."

She passed a hand over her eyes. Then she spoke, very low. "It cannot be."

He was silent for a long moment. Then he took her limp hand in both of his own. "Jacqueline," he said, "tell me your plans."

"Plans?" she said dimly, "I have no plans."

"Do you wish to stay on with Father Flaubert?"

"No. He has been very kind, but no. I cannot stay much longer."

"So where will you go?"

Jacqueline looked at him, her face in tight control. "I am sorry I presumed so much," she said, "but I thought you would help me decide that. I need your help." She paused. "I have come to depend on it."

He felt sorry suddenly, knowing he had unintentionally hurt her, knowing what such a confession cost this proud girl.

"Child, that is why I asked. I care very much about your future. I want to help you, if I am able. But I cannot order you about; I cannot tell you to go here or there. You must decide what you want. Then I can help you."

Her face had lost its tightness and she looked like a child. "You will not leave me to fend for myself?" she asked.

"God is always with you, child. But no, this frail human will not leave until you are ready." Brother Giles smiled at her, and his smile was like the sun, giving warmth.

"Think upon what you must do, Jacqueline. There is no hurry. Ask your own soul what is right. It will not fail you.

Chapter 34

The mist parted and she could see people running, shouting something. A battle! She could hear a booming that sounded like thunder and see the air grow thick with black smoke. She was running away to hide, and suddenly Guillaume was there, running beside her, holding her hand. Though they were in great danger, she felt glad to be with him. They ran until they saw the spire of a church rising before them through the smoke. They went in, feeling relieved to be in a place of refuge.

Inside, safe, they clung to each other. The smell of incense was sweet, and priests were chanting. The melody was soothing, comforting. She smiled, feeling secure. Her love was with her and they had come home…

Jacqueline stared into the dark for a long time after waking. She had not wanted to awaken, to realize it had been but a dream. Guillaume's image was so close to her, crystal clear in her mind. She seemed to feel his lingering presence, as though he had been with her in reality, and not only in a dream.

She tried to think of what it meant. The church…coming home. Deep in the dark of night, she could not deny to herself what she had denied to Brother Giles. Her dream was still with her. If she could not have Guillaume, then she wanted what she had chosen before knowing him- or rather, what had chosen her. To become a nun. The thought settled calmly into her brain. She could neither fight it nor accept it. She had to wait to see where the thought would take her.

After many minutes she drifted back to sleep again, this time deep and black, unmarred by dreams.

How odd, thought the old nun, *that the realization of where I belonged, which should have brought peace, brought a kind of despair. For I could not believe that God would ever accept me after my sin, and I would again lose that which I valued above all.* And another thought too had come, unbidden; that the love of a man was sweet, and she would never again know it. But she had lost that when she lost her love. The morning after that long-ago dream had brought a further despair, the old nun remembered, for it had brought the last news she had of her family.

Upon awakening, the sickness of despair washed over Jacqueline. How dare she cling to this dream? She would never be accepted as a holy woman. No, she had lost that too. Best to put the idea from her mind. Best to leave this place, where they had been so kind, best to leave Brother Giles with his disturbing insights, and go far away.

She was still mulling over this plan when she went to the marketplace later that morning to buy food for Father Flaubert's household. Mistress Leroy disliked the task, and so had delegated it to Jacqueline, who liked to lose her thoughts in the melee of market day. But this day her thoughts could not be shaken, and something was to happen to put her mind in even greater turmoil.

As she approached the marketplace, she saw an unusual sight for this small and poor town. An entourage of very fine horses and goods was gathered in the square. Such horses were not the plodding farm horses occasionally seen in this small town, but delicate, finely bred. She thought of the stables in her father's castle, and felt a weakness descend upon her. She turned to move away, but the crowd was too thick. Everyone was there to see the fine sight that their town rarely offered. She heard people whispering. Suddenly she heard a name spoken, a name from her past, and she thought for a moment that her heart would cease beating in her breast.

"Lord Courcy."

The name rang in her ears. She started, coming aware all of a sudden, and tried to turn and run, but people pressed around her. Their faces swam before her. "Let me through!" she gasped, panicking.

"Here, child," said a woman sharply, as Jacqueline ran into her. "Have a care." Then she noticed Jacqueline's face and said, not unkindly, "Why, what is wrong?"

"Is it—who does this belong to?" Jacqueline asked, indicating the entourage with her hand.

"A man named Lord Courcy, so I have heard," the woman answered.

"I must get away."

"Are you in trouble, girl?"

"No!" Jacqueline cried. She slipped away from the woman, into the crowd again, not wanting to answer curious questions. She must not give her identity away. For, in her panic, she believed that her father had changed his mind. Surely he wanted to call her back, to marry her to Lord Courcy after all. And surely that was why he was in this small town; he was traveling the length of England looking for her. Surely someone would tell him of the girl at Father Flaubert's, the girl who wandered in as a pilgrim of sorts, and stayed. She would not return there. She must go to Brother Giles.

She was exhausted when she reached the monastery walls, for she had run much of the way. She stopped to rest, then knocked at the gates.

"Yes, what is it?" a kindly-sounding brown-garbed figure came into view.

"I must see Brother Giles," she gasped.

"He is at prayer. A monk at prayer cannot be disturbed."

"Oh, please. Please, I am desperate!"

The monk gazed at her for a moment, then nodded assent and opened the gates. He led her to a visitor's chamber and bade her be seated. In minutes, Brother Giles appeared and came through the door. He saw her distress immediately and went to her, taking her hand.

"Jacqueline, what is wrong?"

"I am afraid," she said.

"What has happened?"

She hesitated then. If she told him, he would know who she was. Would he send her back? Would he tell her it would be the best thing for her? She looked into his deep brown eyes, his warm and honest eyes. No, he would not betray her.

"Someone has come to the town," she said. "It is a man I once knew. His name is Lord Courcy. My father wanted to betroth me to him. I fear he has come for me. I do not want to go back. I have not lived through this pain for naught! I will not go back and betray Guillaume's memory!"

She shook her head violently, as though to give further weight to her words. But Brother Giles spoke sharply.

"Stop! Jacqueline, stop. Listen to me. Lord Courcy has not come for you."

She gazed at him as his words sank in. "How do you know this?"

"Lord Courcy is merely passing through on his way to your father's castle. He is betrothed to your sister, Marie."

She looked at him, shocked.

"Forgive me, Jacqueline. I know who you are. I have heard this news from some of the brothers who were at the marketplace today. The betrothal of the rich Lord Courcy to the Lady Marie Bonel is common knowledge there. But Lord Courcy does not know you are here. No one knows."

"How long have you known who I was?" she asked. Strangely, she seemed to have known all along that he knew her. Had not he seen into her very soul? Of course he knew her name. She felt a calm descend upon her. Brother Giles would never betray her.

"I have always known," he said, and smiled, for he saw her peaceful look. She did not even ask him how he had come to know. It seemed right that he knew.

"How is my sister?" she asked. "Do you know about that?"

"She is pleased with the arrangement, so I have heard."

"My father…my father must be pleased," she said, then choked on the words. "I cannot think of it," she whispered. "I hate him bitterly…may God forgive me." She turned away from Brother Giles, and so did not see the joy on his face. It would have startled her. Should a monk rejoice because she hated her father? But Brother Giles rejoiced in his heart because Jacqueline had asked God's forgiveness. She was regaining her lost faith. All else would come in time, he knew.

The old nun woke suddenly, then laughed at herself. *I am falling asleep at odd moments,* she thought. *Like a baby. We return to infancy in our old age.* Then she recalled her earlier thoughts. She had been thinking of Brother Giles. She thought of him often lately. He had set her feet on the path. But he would not be proud of her in one thing. That even now, in her great age, with her life so near its end- even now, she had not yet forgiven her father. That sin would forever be on her soul. She was not even able to pray about it anymore

Chapter 35

The news of Marie's coming marriage was the last that Jacqueline ever heard of her family. Brother Giles had, of course, been right. Lord Courcy had no inkling of her whereabouts, nor did he care. He had merely spent the night in town on the way to the estate of his betrothed. Jacqueline put thought of the episode from her mind. Her family was no longer her family. She was alone in the world. She had to exist on her own, without yearning for what might have been. But the doubt and questions about her future still lingered.

Yet she had entered a new phase. She felt confused still. The ache of Guillaume's loss was still, always, with her and she could not believe in the goodness of God. But there was something in the back of her mind, some suppressed thought, that stirred a great restlessness in her. She only knew that she could not be still. She put great energy into her daily work, and when she had free time, she took to walking to the edge of the woods and back. Doing this, she could not help but remember the vision in the wood so long ago, the vision that had come in her other life. Fall was in full color now. The leaves were shaded in blazing reds and golds and russets. The air was sharp and crisp. The world was so beautiful. How could there be such pain and evil in such a beautiful world? Something caught in Jacqueline's throat. She loved the world, loved the beauty around her. She loved it and that love spread warmth inside her. It was such joy to love something, she who had been so wounded by loving. It was so good to sit on the fading grass wrapped in her warm cloak, and to love the trees and the blue sky and the sun.

She sat for a long time. And as she sat, thoughts of Guillaume came to her. Usually she pushed aside such thoughts in a deep violent pain, but now she let them come, let them wash over her as they would. She saw him as she first knew him, holding her horse Padgett's reins, gazing at her so intently. She remembered the day they had ridden in the woods and she told him of her vision. She remembered his low voice, his words of love. She remembered what it was like to love him, the passion and power of it. Memory burned inside her, and pain grew and swelled inside her. But she did not push it away this time, and she did not weep. She let the memory come, these thoughts of her beloved Guillaume, and memory blended with the beauty of the day. She felt love swell within her. She had loved him purely, truly, with her whole heart. Her love had made him happy. And, though it had given her such terrible pain, it had made her happy too. He had loved her. Perhaps somewhere he still loved her.

And a strange thing happened. In all the months since he had gone from the world, Jacqueline had not felt joy. Now she felt a small stirring of joy within her. Guillaume had loved her, and loved her still. *He would not have wanted me to give up my dream,* she thought. *I have lost Guillaume, my love, but I still have myself. And God- do I not still have God? How could this day be so beautiful, if there was no God?*

Later that night the small elusive joy that had stirred within Jacqueline was gone. The dullness of daily life, the bitterness of her dependence on charity, was with her again. But one thing was changed. She knew that she had to go and see Brother Giles; she knew what it was that she would tell him.

Chapter 36

She did not go to see him, though, because he came to her the very next day. As she labored at her morning chores, Mistress Leroy came to her and told her that Brother Giles was there and wished to speak with her. She was surprised. "So early in the day," she said, but Mistress Leroy merely shrugged. She was used to the odd ways of holy men.

Jacqueline smoothed her rumpled housedress and went to greet Brother Giles. Before she had a chance to question him, he spoke of his purpose.

"I dreamed of you last night, Jacqueline."

"Of what," she said, surprised again.

"In my dream you seemed somehow at peace. I felt- I hoped you would have something to tell me. So I came."

She could no longer be stunned by his insight. She answered calmly, "You are right. Again, you have read my mind."

And he smiled, a smile like the sunrise.

"Jacqueline," he said, his voice glad, "Tell me."

She smiled an answering smile, very slight, but it warmed his heart. "I would like," she said, in a voice so low it was almost a whisper, "to enter a convent." She had been looking down at her hands as she spoke; now she looked up at him, her eyes full of questions.

"Yes. God wills it." He took her hands. And her questions were answered.

The voice raised in song filled the small church, seemed to swell its rafters and set its walls to trembling. The voices together were strong, melodious, joyous. The old nun's voice was weak now, but still true. They were celebrating a special mass to welcome a new nun into the fold. She had been so happy to at last take her final vows. Her head was bowed, and her hands folded, but a small smile rested on her lips, as though it had permanently settled there. Now she was one of them. God's chosen. Every nun there had recalled her own vows that day. The old nun too had remembered. It was so long ago! But she remembered well.

She had that same night spoken to Father Flaubert about her decision. He was overcome with joy for her. In his hearty, very human and practical way, he said that he wished her well. He called God's blessings upon her, loudly and with gladness, and spoke to her of people who would be traveling soon, suggesting she go with them to a convent near a town three days travel away. Jacqueline was glad at last to go to bed. Exhausted by the day, by her work, and by the decision she had finally made, she slept soundly.

Two days later in the early morning Mistress Leroy pressed a packet of food into her hands, and surprised Jacqueline with a quick hug. "Take care, dearie," she whispered. "God go with you." Jacqueline turned to join her fellow travelers, who had arrived the evening before. And so she set out on the journey to her new life.

Final Chapter

And so the day came when everything changed.

A visitor came, a visit to this quiet nunnery that rarely saw outsiders. There was a commotion in the yard below as the old nun sat at her window. She looked in amazement and curiosity as a small retinue of horses rode in, scattering the chickens in the yard in four directions as they ran to escape the beating hoofs. She saw two of the nuns come out of the chapter house to meet the horsemen. The horses were led away and all was quiet for a time.

Presently a knock came on her door and one of the young nuns entered, softly speaking, the words seeming almost disembodied, entities in themselves; "Sister, you have a visitor. The abbess has given her consent for you to meet with him." The old nun's curiosity transformed into an emotion that had been buried for decades; fear.

She was still for a long moment, though her heart was beating wildly and her breath seemed caught in her lungs. Then, she rose. She took the young nun's offered arm and they went slowly down the stairs, down the long corridor, to the visitor's room, so rarely used.

The old nun looked up at the tall young man who stood before her and gasped. A cry came from her throat, and then a name. "Antoine!" For it was her brother who stood there, looking as young as he had the day she had left, never to return. Her brother, who had betrayed her. Her brother, whom she loved.

The young nun who held her arm appeared alarmed. "Please sit, Sister." She led the old nun to a chair. The young man, his countenance soft, was speaking, but at first she could not hear. She sat and her fear lifted like a cloud, and she saw him more clearly.

"Sister," he said, then "Aunt. It is so wonderful to see you. I have been searching for you for a long time. Allow me to introduce myself. I am your great nephew. I am your sister Joan's grandson, the child of her eldest daughter, Melisende. I am Robert Huxley."

The old nun started at the name. Robert! The name of her long-gone baby brother. Robert! This was happening too swiftly, she could not take it in. Then she composed herself, and nodded softly to the young nun, who respectfully retreated, a question in her eyes. "I am fine," the old nun told her. "I will speak to this young man. I would hear his story."

When the young nun had left the room the old nun turned to Robert. "How is it that you have found me?" she questioned softly. The real question in her heart was *"Why have you found me? What is it that you want that you have brought me back to such a painful time? To memories that have become hazy and distant with age?"*

He moved forward, taking her wrinkled hands in his large ones. She started for a moment and almost pulled away. She was a nun, not to be touched by any man. But his eyes bore into hers, intense hazel eyes, so like her sister's that she could not move. "Aunt," he said, "My grandmother never forgot you. Since I was a very little child, she told me about you, and how you had to leave the castle one day, never to return. I did not learn more about why until I was older, of course. She implored me to find you one day. She told me that her family had tried, but you had disappeared. But she never forgot. She and your sister Marie never forgot."

The tears were burning her eyes then to hear those names from so long ago. Joan. Marie. Her dearest sisters. How she had loved them! How she had been torn from them, never to see them again. She almost feared to ask the next question.

"Are they...are they still alive?"

"My Aunt Marie has gone to her maker some seven years past. But my grandmother still lives."

She felt a stillness come into her heart. Marie. She bowed her head and said a small prayer for her beloved sister. Then she turned her eyes again to her great nephew's. He went on with his story.

"My grandmother never gave up on finding you. She had implored her father- your father- and brothers to look for you shortly after you left. But they were unsuccessful. They..."

The old nun interrupted in her shocked surprise. "But they are the ones who banished me. They hated me. They wanted me gone, they wished me dead. They are the ones..." And it seemed that in that moment she was back, back at the horror of losing Guillaume so violently, at the hands of her father and brothers. And one of those brother's visages was in front of her now.

"You look just like my brother, Antoine."

"Yes," Robert said, and he smiled. "I have always been told so." He went on. "Your father and brothers did not hate you. They mourned your loss. They were sorry that they had done what they had done." The old nun stared at him. He continued, "Your father regretted what he had done for the rest of his life. He became very ill not two years later. On his deathbed he implored his sons to find you. They tried. My great uncles Antoine and Louis, kept trying to find you. They asked at all the great castles, they questioned the nobility they knew. They swallowed their pride and searched for you. It never occurred to them that you had not disappeared into the nobility from whence you came, but another place altogether. It was my grandmother who thought of where you might be. Her brothers did not believe her. But she told me where to look. She told me of your old dream."

Again, the old nun was Jacqueline again, lost, wandering, then finally coming to this place where she had known peace. Now again, she was feeling lost, hearing that nothing was as she had thought, that her father had been sorry, that her brothers who had betrayed her had searched for her. "Do my brothers still live?" she whispered.

"No. My great uncle Antoine was killed in the crusades, fighting with King Richard. My great uncle Louis was killed later in the same war. They had both gone after your father died and served many times before dying heroically. Neither ever married, but they were close to all of us children when we were young. Your younger brother Ralf became lord after your father and other brothers were gone. He married and had five children, but he too is gone these past fifteen years."

She had so many questions, crowding each other in her mind, fearful of the answers, yet feeling an aliveness she had not known since the days before, the time before the horror. How many children did her sisters have? How many grandchildren? Where were all of them, what had they done with the rest of their lives after she had gone? But one thing remained elusive in her mind. She could not yet ponder what he had told her about her father. He had been sorry. He had regretted his rash act. He had wanted to find her and bring her home.

The old nun and her great-nephew sat and talked. They talked for many hours. Sometimes she rested and was quiet, and he waited. Then she would speak again. Sometimes she would even doze, then awaken and see her brother Antoine's face before her. She smiled, happy to see her brother again at long last, until she realized this was quite another young man before her, and she would ask Robert a new question. Finally the day was done, the sun was lowering in the sky, and Robert said that he would leave with his men. But he promised to return.

"It has been so wonderful to meet you, Aunt," he told her, his young voice pleased and proud. "I knew that I would find you. I wanted to give that to my grandmother. I will ride back and give her this great news tomorrow."

When he had gone, the old nun was helped back to her tower room. She sat staring out of the window at the darkening world, barely comprehending what had just happened. She felt a whirl of emotions, emotions she had thought gone forever; wild joy, surprise, sorrow. And another- love. She felt enormous love for the young man who was her great-nephew, this young man who so resembled her brother. She felt great love for her family, so long ago lost. She saw her father's face and all she felt was love. All the other emotions whirled and spiraled in her breast and became only one emotion, this great love that she had for all of these people so long gone, and for her beloved Guillaume as well.

The old nun sat for many hours as the darkness overcame the earth. She heard the gentle sounds of night outside her window. She dozed lightly in her chair, perhaps; she was not certain. Would she really see her sister, her cherished Joan, again? And perhaps her other nieces and nephews, those born of the ones she had loved so long ago, and their children as well? It was almost beyond imagining.

The hours of the night passed as she sat, contemplating. Then there came a hush. The sounds of night seemed to cease, though the world was still dark. The love in her heart seemed to swell and grow even larger, so that it expanded beyond the walls of her small room, beyond the convent, to the fields and woods and far away across the land. Without warning it became light, as though day had come all suddenly. But the light was not the light of day. It was a blue light, a soft blue, with a golden center and a white light within that. And within that light Jacqueline could see a face, a form. She saw his gentle features, his youth, saw his light brown hair. She saw the green of his eyes. He smiled at her and the light grew brighter, so bright that it surrounded her and enfolded her. And then Guillaume held out his hand.

The End

www.ingramcontent.com/pod-product-compliance
Lightning Source LLC
Chambersburg PA
CBHW052012170626
46808CB00007B/2894